THE BUILDER

CJ MORROW

Tamarillas Press

This book is written in British English.

Cover image: stuartbur/istockphoto.com
Cover design: ©CJ Morrow 2023

ISBN: 978-1-913807-34-4

For the sisters who are doing it for themselves!
They know who they are.

Other books by CJ MORROW

Women's Fiction/Romantic Comedy:
Save the Date
Escape to Christmas Cottage
It's Pamela Rigby Actually
Sooo Not Looking for a Man
We can Work it Out
Little Mishaps and Big Surprises
Mermaid Hair and I Don't Care
Blame it on the Onesie
A Onesie is not just for Christmas

Psychological Thriller:
Never Leaves Me
Kill For You
The Builder

Fantasy:
The Finder
The Illusionist
The Sister
The Family

One

I used to feel sorry for Micky.

I don't now.

Looking back I realise that the signs were there even at the beginning. The first time I saw Micky leaning on the bar in The Carpenters I was immediately drawn to him. He was tall, dark-haired and tanned. I learned, as the evening wore on, that he'd just come back from a riotous two weeks in Ibiza. A tan suited him. It went with his eyes. Made them shine.

'Hello, Callie,' he said after we'd been introduced. He twinkled those deep brown eyes at me.

I smiled and nodded back as I pulled his pint. I wasn't shy but I'd met enough of his sort before. Charming. Slick. Drinkers.

He was, so John the landlord told me, a regular. He and Jez always sat at the end of the bar. They weren't rowdy, they weren't trouble; they were a regular income for the pub, a reliable one. I had to keep them sweet and keep the drinks flowing.

It was the start of my third week working behind

the bar and Micky's holiday explained why his mate Jez had spent the last two weeks looking so glum. Now that Micky was back Jez had cheered right up. He was grinning and laughing as Micky regaled him with his Ibizan exploits. I remember that night with fondness.

They were an odd-looking couple, not that they were a couple, Micky made it clear to me that first night that they were just mates, drinking buddies.

Micky Fisher was a charmer. He had a ready smile, a quick wit, an ability to make whoever he was talking to feel like the most important person in the world. He certainly charmed me. By the end of the evening I'd accepted a date invitation from him. And I couldn't wait.

Now look at me.

I'm trudging along carrying a heaving shopping bag in each hand, at least I'm evened out, weighted equally on both sides. My handbag is slung diagonally across my body and slaps against my heavily pregnant belly with every step. I really should have been more careful; having a baby so quickly into our marriage wasn't the best of ideas. But we are where we are. I'm looking forward to meeting the little man jumping about inside me. And after he arrives, I have plans.

Ours was a whirlwind romance, me and Micky Fisher. We'd been out a few times, had a few dinners and gone back to my tatty studio flat and slept together. To be fair Micky was not a bad lover, definitely better than the few I'd had already. And he was keen to look after me. After our third or fourth date he told me that he didn't like the way men ogled me in the pub.

I laughed.

'Don't laugh,' he said. 'I mean it. They leer at you, especially those hardened drinkers. If you've noticed it's a boozers' pub, not a pub grub pub.'

I smiled. He was certainly right about it being a boozers' pub, but I knew that when I took the job. No food was served, not even cheesy chips or a limp club sandwich. The only edibles were crisps, peanuts and pork scratchings. We sold them rarely because proper drinkers aren't that interested in edibles. If sales, beer sales especially, were slow, John would break out a packet or two of peanuts, tip them into a bowl and have me wander around offering customers, or punters as he slyly called them, a little handful. He knew only too well that the salt would make them thirstier, and they'd be more inclined to take a few salty snacks from me than him.

'It's okay,' I said to Micky. 'I'm fine.'

'No, you're not. I don't want you working there when we're married. I want you home in the evenings with me.'

I'd stopped what I was doing and stared at him. Married? Did he just say married? Was this some kind of cackhanded proposal?

Even now I'm not sure if he meant to say it or if it just slipped out, but he could tell by my face that I'd heard the word. The M word.

I just stood and blinked at him; I must have looked as though I was malfunctioning. In all my years of dating I'd never had the M word said to me and I never really expected to. I was thirty-one, still thought I had plenty of time and was happy flitting from one man to the next, or not if none took my fancy.

'Did you hear what I said?' he asked, his face taking on a soppy look.

'I think so.'

'Not very romantic, sorry about that, but I'm asking you to marry me.' He grinned then. 'What do you say?'

Wow, I was flattered. I really liked Micky. He obviously really liked me. But marriage? It was way too early for that, surely. I just couldn't answer because I was so taken aback.

He dropped down onto one knee and still I continued staring and blinking.

'Trying to romantic the moment up,' he said. 'What do you say? Callie, my darling, will you marry me?'

What could I say? I liked him, really liked him. He made me feel special. I wanted to continue spending time with him and if I said no that would be it. Micky Fisher wasn't the sort of man to shrug off a marriage refusal and carry on as before. If I said no, I'd lose him. I'd have nobody, just like usual.

'Okay,' I said, feeling shy. 'I will.'

'Great.' He jumped up, wrapped his arms around me and gave me a bear hug, lifting me off my feet in the process. 'Haven't got a ring,' he said. 'Because I really didn't plan this. But who doesn't love a bit of spontaneity? He kissed me then, hard, before adding, 'Anyway, waste of money really, we can use the money to put a deposit on a house.'

What? A marriage and a proper home all in one go? Things were finally looking up for me. I hadn't had a proper home since Mum died when I was sixteen. It had always been just the two of us and after she'd gone I'd been pushed into a hostel for teenagers because there wasn't anywhere else for me to go. I wasn't going to be allowed to stay in the little two-bed social housing flat that we'd called home for the past couple of years, so that was it. I became nomadic.

Now, suddenly, here was Micky offering me a life and a home.

'I don't suppose you've got any savings?' he said, a hopeful tone to his voice.

'You must be joking.'

'Yeah, didn't think so. Never mind. I've got enough for a deposit, providing you don't insist on an engagement ring.'

I'd have loved an engagement ring, but a house was definitely a better offer, so I shrugged, smiled, shook my head and wrapped my arms around Micky Fisher.

'We can have a small wedding,' he said. 'I don't get on with my family, haven't seen any of 'em for years so they won't be coming. What about you?'

'No,' I said, feeling rather sad. 'It was just me and Mum.' I'd already told him about my mum so he knew I was an orphan at sixteen.

'Cool, because big weddings are another waste of money, aren't they?'

'Yes,' I agreed. To be fair I'd never imagined

myself waltzing down the aisle in a flowing gown with bridesmaids and pageboys so I wasn't pining for that. I'd never imagined myself walking down the aisle at all.

'Now we need to get you a proper job that pays better than that pub and doesn't involve drunkards leering at you.' He seemed to forget that he was one of those leering drunkards.

Before I knew it I was going for an interview in our local superstore and after a little bit of training I soon found myself manning the self-service tills. If I heard *unexpected item in the bagging area* just once an hour it was a good day. But at least I was paid more than in the pub and I could work extra shifts to help towards getting a mortgage.

We found, or rather Micky found, the house we live in now, and before I knew it I was signing papers, handing over my wage slips as proof of income and suddenly I was the joint owner of my first proper home in fifteen years. It was surreal.

The house was okay, not stunning, not beautiful, but okay. Detached with two bedrooms and, according to Micky, potential.

'It needs work, Callie,' Micky said, the first night we moved in. 'Bit of decorating, bit of a tidy up, you'll see. Jez is a dab hand at wallpapering, or so he tells me.'

But Jez wasn't a dab hand at anything other than propping up a bar in a boozers' pub, so his efforts were soon dismissed and we blundered about ourselves. It was fun at first, stripping the hideous wallpaper and painting the rooms. But it soon became apparent that no amount of paint or wallpaper would solve the problem of the miniscule, tatty kitchen or the collapsing lean-to beyond it, laughingly referred to as a conservatory by the estate agent.

'It needs proper work, Callie,' Micky said. 'If you do a few more shifts at the supermarket, maybe a couple of evenings, we'll soon have the money saved up and we can get a new kitchen, and get that godawful lean-to knocked down.'

Dutifully I did as I was asked, because, after all, this was my home too.

I never asked Micky where he was when I was working evenings on the self-service tills; I didn't want to upset the atmosphere in our home which was, for the most part, convivial. Of course I knew exactly where he was, in the same place he'd been when I met him. I never suggested that he cut down on his boozing and save the money, maybe I should have.

We got married in a tiny ceremony late one Friday afternoon. There was just us, John the pub landlord, and Jez. If we hadn't needed witnesses I think Micky wouldn't even have invited them. He was really keen for us to marry, said it kept everything neat and tidy and that since he was now forty, it was the right time for him. He said he'd even put my name on his 'death in service' forms at work. I didn't really know what that was but he explained that if he died, I'd get three times his salary. He worked in a warehouse, the biggest food warehouse in the South West he told me. He was a supervisor. He was very proud of that.

He'd been there twenty years, worked his way up.

Then it happened, I found out I was pregnant. I bought the test in the supermarket pharmacy on my way home after my extra evening shift. Micky wasn't in so I did the first one on my own, saving the other until he came back. I didn't know what his reaction would be so I needed to broach the subject carefully.

I wasn't exactly sure what my own reaction was either.

'Hey, Callie,' he said, when he mis-stepped through the door. 'Give me a hug.' He was drunk, happy, but drunk.

I thought of the extra four hours I'd worked that evening while he was throwing back booze with his mate Jez. I felt the stirrings of annoyance. I shrugged off his hug.

'Hey, what's up with my little wifey?'

I looked at his drunken, happy face, he still looked hot even in that state. 'I think I might be pregnant,' I said, my tone so much flatter than I'd planned.

'What? No?'

I nodded my head to confirm my announcement.

'Have you done a test?'

'Yes.'

'You need to get another one, they can be wrong.'

'I've got a second one, they come two in a box. Shall I do it now?'

He slumped into a chair. 'Yeah, I think you should. And bring it down to show me.'

I traipsed up to the bathroom, performed the act and took the evidence back to Micky.

'Micky,' I called, my voice loud because he'd nodded off.

'Yeah, yeah. Well?'

I waved the stick at him.

'Well,' he said, 'ain't that a thing?' Then he closed his eyes again and nodded off, so I left him there sleeping off his evening booze up and I went to bed.

Hours later he staggered up the stairs, banged about in the bathroom then flopped into bed beside me. He was soon snoring and it kept me awake but I couldn't wake *him*, no matter how many times I elbowed him in the ribs.

The thing with Micky is he never gets a hangover. How can that be? He drinks more in an evening that I could drink in a week. Not that I'm much of a drinker, I never had the money for it when I was the age when most people develop the taste so I'd never really got into alcohol. And certainly not like Micky. Maybe that's the trick to never getting a hangover, keep the alcohol topped up to such a level that you're never really sober. Maybe that's what Micky does.

In the morning, after I'd picked his clothes up off the bathroom floor and sorted them out, I went downstairs to make a cup of tea in our tiny, tatty kitchen. Minutes later Micky was by my side.

'Callie,' he said, grabbing the mug of tea I'd just made for myself. 'Had such a weird dream, dreamt you were pregnant.' He laughed.

'I am,' I said, flicking on the kettle to bring the water back to the boil for my own mug of tea.

He blinked at me several times before a great big,

stupid grin spread across his face.

'Yeah?' he questioned.

'Yeah,' I confirmed, smiling shyly.

'Great,' he said, the grin getting bigger. 'We need to get cracking then. Jez has a mate who knows someone who's cheap.'

My face fell, what the hell was he talking about? I dreaded to think.

'We need to get the house extended. We've only got two bedrooms and one of those is a box room. We need a master suite for us and a bigger kitchen. It'll be great. Might mean a few more extra shifts in the supermarket though.' He did a little mock wince then grinned again.

'And maybe some overtime at work for you,' I added, trying to sound cheerful.

'There's no overtime,' he said, his tone sharp. 'If they want extra work doing they bring in cheap agency workers on minimum wage. Bastards.'

I wanted to suggest that he cut down his boozy nights but I didn't.

So here we are, more extra shifts for me, seven months pregnant and the house a bloody building site.

Yep, once this baby is born and I've got my strength back I'll be making a few changes.

Two

As I dump the shopping bags on the kitchen worktop I can hear Micky's voice. He's laughing, and lecturing.

Outside he's talking to the builder, his arms gesticulating wildly. They stand with their backs to me. From this angle they look very similar, both tall, both broad-shouldered. It's only as they turn to face each other that the differences are obvious. Micky has a beard, a dark bushy thing that he's grown since we married; the builder is clean shaven. The builder is, I suspect, not British. On the rare occasions when I hear him speak there's a tiny tinge of something interesting in his accent. Other than hello, and thank you when I take him the odd cup of tea, we've had no conversation. I only know that his name is Mick because Micky told me; he thought it was funny. Maybe he's Irish, maybe that's what I'm hearing.

He's been working out there for two weeks now. He's on his own and seems to do everything by hand, no mini-digger to help him. The ground looks hard and I've seen him use a pick axe to break it up before he digs. This is the builder that came by way of Jez, the one who is cheap. Not, we've since found out, that Jez has ever met him. Jez is so full of bullshit. Mick the builder works hard, even I can see that. He's demolished and removed the hideous lean-to already and started on the footings for the extension. I think it's rather grand the extension. A giant kitchen just like the ones Micky's seen online plus a master suite above it. The plans took a while to go through – someone else Micky found cheap – but once they passed Mick started promptly. Micky says it'll all be finished before the baby's born. I really cannot see that. I only have eight more weeks at most.

'Great job, mate,' I hear Micky say to the builder, before he slaps him on the back. He heads for the kitchen with a half-smile on his face until he sees me.

'Wasn't expecting you home yet,' he says.

'Hello to you too.'

'Aren't you working an extra tonight?'

'I was. I started it but got sent home.'

Alarm fills his eyes. 'Why? Not going to sack you, are they?'

'No, of course not. Why would you think that? I didn't feel well. My ankles have swollen.' I look down at my puffy feet. So does Micky.

'You've always had fat ankles.'

I don't reply because I can tell from his mood that he's spoiling for a row. Lately we've had a few rows. Though none about his drinking. I start to unpack the shopping I've hauled all the way from the supermarket, swollen ankles or not.

'These are warm,' Micky says, snatching a pack of

beers from my hands.

I don't reply. What is there to say? He stuffs all four cans in the freezer which means he intends to drink them this as soon as he can.

'I'm going out later,' he says.

'Okay. I'm probably going to go and lie down. I rang my midwife and she said to put my feet up.'

He gives me a withering look.

'Well don't get used to it. Things aren't looking so good for me either.'

'What do you mean?'

Is there something wrong with him, something I've missed?

'Yeah, well I wasn't going to say anything but you might as well know there's talk of redundancies at work.'

'Oh.' I slump down on the stool we keep in the kitchen, the one I stand on to reach things on the top of the wall cupboards. We keep a lot of stuff on top of the cupboards because there's nowhere else.

'Yeah, we find out on Monday whose job is at risk then there's this whole process, well…' He shrugs.

'I'm so sorry.' I haul myself up and approach him for a hug but he steps away. 'You'll be okay.'

'Let's hope so for all our sakes.' He studies me for a moment or two. 'You should go and lie down, we don't want anything happening to my son, do we?'

I go to the sink, run the cold tap, fill a glass, then take it upstairs with me. I'm so tired I feel as though I could sleep for a year. As I turn at the top of the stairs I hear Micky opening the freezer door. I stop. I wait. Then I hear the unmistakeable sound of a ring pull tab. That beer can't be very cold yet.

I wander into the spare bedroom, the small one at the back of the house. We haven't decorated it for the baby because Micky says the extension will be finished by then and we'll move in there and the baby can have our room at the front. We have, however, been buying baby things and keeping them in this room. There's a cot, dismantled and propped against the wall. There's a baby bath, a crib, and little bits and pieces I've bought with my staff discount; tiny little clothes and packs of nappies.

It's stuffy in the room and I open the window a little. The sound attracts the attention of the builder who looks up at me. He smiles. I smile back, then wander back towards our bedroom, desperate for my bed.

I'm kicking off my shoes and I've just pulled off my top when Micky bursts in, his face like thunder.

'What's going on?' he roars.

'I don't know. What's wrong?'

'I saw *him* smile up at you. Were you parading around like that?' He points at me and suddenly I feel very vulnerable in my bra, which I admit has become a bit tight of late.

'Of course not.'

'You sure about that? I've seen you looking at him.'

I shake my head and pull the bedcovers back, pull out the voluminous nighty from under the pillow that I've taken to wearing. I'm just so desperate to get inside that bed and close my eyes.

'Is that why you came home early? You didn't

expect me to be here, did you?'

'Really, Micky? Do you think any man would want me like this? You certainly don't.'

He stares at me for a long second, then shrugs, turns and stomps back downstairs.

I wake with a start, the urge to use the toilet overriding my need for sleep. I stumble along to the bathroom but the door is shut. Damn it. I can hear the shower running which makes me want to use the toilet even more. At least when all this work is finished we'll have a second bathroom and a downstairs toilet. I cross my legs and will myself not to think about it.

I stumble back and stop again at the spare room. It's chilly up here now so I go in and close the window. The builder has gone, his day's work done.

'If you're looking for lover boy he's gone,' Micky says from the doorway. He's towelling himself dry.

'What?'

'He's finished for the day.'

I choose to ignore him. 'Have you finished in the bathroom?'

'Yeah,' he says. He doesn't step aside as I move to pass him. I can smell more than beer on his breath. He's probably started on the whisky. Sometimes I think I only work so he can drink heavily.

'Can I get past then? I'm wetting myself.'

'Charming,' he says, moving away and heading into our bedroom.

When I come out of the bathroom he's fully

dressed and hovering on the landing.

'You going out?' I ask, trying to sound casual.

'Yeah. Said I was. What of it?'

I shrug and shake my head slightly as if to say, 'nothing to me.'

'I had to make beans on toast,' he says.

'Oh, right.' There's no point in asking if he's made me any, or thought to bring it upstairs for me.

'Yeah, because you didn't cook any dinner.'

'I didn't feel well.'

'Doesn't matter now.'

'No.' I move past him, keen to lie down in bed until he's gone out.

I do wonder where the Micky Fisher I first met has gone? He's no longer the charmer and he no longer makes me feel as though I'm the only person in the world that matters to him. If anything, I no longer matter at all, his only concern is his unborn son, and I'm starting to have doubts about how much he cares about him.

Months ago, when I wasn't so very pregnant as I am now, I asked him why he had become so grumpy. He said it was the responsibility of family life, the worry about the extension getting done in time, being a proper grown-up. He said he didn't want to end up like his own father, a drunken bully.

He's not doing too well on that one. Not that he'd ever hit me. Well, he hasn't so far.

He's still waiting at the top of the stairs, watching me as I push at our bedroom door.

'This bloody extension,' he says, sighing. 'It'll be the death of me. Especially if I lose my job.'

I turn, see that his face is screwed up as though he's trying to work something out.

'You won't,' I say, trying to sound convincing, reassuring. 'If you're worried about the money maybe we should just stop it. That old tatty lean-to has gone, that was dangerous. Just pay the builder for that and leave it as it is.'

'House isn't big enough.'

'We've got two bedrooms. That's fine. Babies don't need a lot of space to start off with.'

He gives me a withering look. 'Too bloody late,' he mutters. 'You should have said this weeks ago.'

'Why's it too late?'

'I've already paid him.'

'What? The full amount?'

'No, course not but I've had to give him some cash. He was cheap for a reason, you know.'

'I don't know. I don't understand.'

'No, you wouldn't.'

'Then tell me.'

'He doesn't have a good credit rating with the builder's merchant so has to pay as he goes.' He's sneering at me now.

'Okay. But he hasn't bought anything from the builder's merchant, has he? There aren't any materials here. Are there?'

'He's had to order stuff in advance, pay for it up front. Shut up about it now, we're committed. We need that extension.'

'We don't,' I say, stepping towards him. 'We can manage if it's causing you worry. We can just stop. Cut our losses. Anyway, I don't see how much longer I can work extra shifts, it's exhausting me.'

'Oh yeah,' he says. 'Make it about you. Always about you.'

'That's not fair.'

'Na na na,' he says, which I take to be his imitation of me. It infuriates me, emboldens me.

'Or maybe you could cut down on the drinking, not go to the pub most nights.' I know I'm pushing my luck but it has to be said.

'And what about Jez?'

'What about him?'

'He's my mate, we go back a long way. I don't see half as much of him now as I used to before you came on the scene.'

'Nor should you.' I turn away.

'Hey,' he snaps. 'Don't turn away from me when I'm talking to you.' He grabs my wrist.

I stop, turn, look at his hand around my arm. 'Let go.'

'Don't fucking do it then.'

I look at him. See the anger in his eyes. Feel my heart racing. Is this how it starts? Is this when he turns into his own father? A drunkard. A bully.

I may be smaller than him. I may be pregnant. But I won't be bullied. I grew up overnight, became independent overnight when my mum died.

He's still gripping my wrist. He squeezes it tighter.

'Let. Go.'

He smiles, just a little smile, but I know what he's thinking… that he's got me, that I'm weaker than him. Physically I am. I shake my arm. He lets go.

'Drunken wanker,' I say.

I've pushed my luck.

The slap to my face knocks me off my feet.

So this *is* how it starts.

I'm falling down the stairs in slow motion. My arms are flailing. My feet slap against each step but they won't grip.

I think of my unborn son, wonder what it's like for him.

Three

The lights are so bright and there's a searing pain in my back.

'Mrs Fisher, Mrs Fisher, Callie?' Who the hell is that?

'Yeah?'

'Do you know where you are?'

I don't answer because I don't know where I am. It isn't home that's for sure, we don't have any lights this bright.

'My back,' I mumble.

'The anaesthetist is just putting an epidural in for you.'

'What?'

'Just lie still until she's finished.'

'Where am I?'

'You're in hospital.'

'Why?'

'You fell.'

I wait a while before I can say anything because slowly, it's coming back to me. The spat – because that's all it was, wasn't it – at the top of the stairs with Micky?

'My baby? My baby?'

There's a long silence which I know doesn't bode well.

'Callie, Callie, listen to me.' A concerned face comes into focus now. A nurse? A doctor? 'We're just sorting out the epidural, if you can just keep still.'

I wasn't even aware that I wasn't keeping still.

'Am I having the baby now?' I search her face for an answer. She frowns then pats my hand. 'Am I? Is my baby okay?'

'Okay,' a voice says from behind me.

'Callie, the epidural is in and should kick in soon.'

'So, my baby…'

The nurse, doctor, midwife, I don't know what she is, pulls up a chair and sits down. Her face is close to mine.

'Callie, you've had quite a fall and we think you lay unconscious for a while. You're going to be okay; we can't find any serious injuries on you. A few bruises, maybe a concussion.'

I gasp because she isn't mentioning the baby which can mean only one thing. I'm about to ask again but she speaks first.

'Unfortunately baby hasn't survived. You've had a placental abruption and baby didn't get enough oxygen. I'm so sorry.'

'Placental abruption,' I repeat.

'It's where the placenta tears away from the womb.'

I should be screaming, I should be crying, I should be yelling and saying she's wrong. But I don't do any of those things. I just can't take it in. Instead I ask, 'Where's my husband?'

'I'll check for you. He was in A&E getting stitched up.'

'Stitched up?'

'He fell too. Hit his head on the hand rail?'

'Where?'

'On the stairs, when you both tripped on the loose carpet. I'll check if he's back yet.' With that she's gone.

We're home now and it's horrible. I insisted on leaving as soon as I could stand up. They didn't want me to go because of the epidural but I insisted. They were going to put me in a ward with other mothers; mothers with live babies. That would have just been too much, too cruel. They would have liked to give me my own room, a side ward, but the place was full, so they couldn't. So I came home. I made Micky push me in a wheelchair out to a taxi and now, here we are, home. He came in the ambulance with me so he didn't have his car, but he'd probably already drunk too much to drive anyway.

It's not much of a home.

I'm numb and not just from the epidural. My emotions are numbed too. I can't get my head around the fact that my baby is no more especially when I look down at my still enlarged belly. How can he not be safely swimming around in there? But he isn't. I know because I held him. Snuggled his soft little body to mine until it started to stiffen. They said they could get a special cot to keep him cool so that we could spend more time with him but Micky said no. To be honest I was almost past caring by then. What is the point in anything now? My baby is gone, dead.

'Cup of tea, Cal?' Micky's voice is soft yet gravelly. He doesn't look too good himself. There's a big white pad taped to his forehead and he has the beginnings of a black eye. He's told me more than once that's he's had six stitches.

I've had considerably more than that but I wouldn't have minded if my little boy was here, sweet and warm in my arms.

'Tea?' he prompts because I haven't answered.

I shrug and waddle over to the sofa where I lower myself down. I'm wadded up with pads to soak up the bleeding but I couldn't care less if I bleed to death on this sofa right now.

Nothing matters any longer. Nothing. Not me. Not Micky. Not us.

Micky goes out and clatters around in the kitchen. I've no idea what the time is but guess it's late in the day. I glance out of the window looking for the builder's van, but there's no sign of him.

At least we'll be able to stop the extension now; there's absolutely no point to it at all.

Micky comes back with a mug of tea and a plate of biscuits. He puts them down in front of me.

'You need to eat something, Cal,' he says. 'They said at the hospital.'

I can't bring myself to even look at him. If I had somewhere else to go, I'd be gone now. But I don't. So I'll have to bide my time, recover – if that's even possible – then make my plans.

I start to cry and Micky flops down on the sofa next to me and puts his arms around me and hugs me tight. I let him because it's the only source of comfort available at the moment.

'It hurts me too, Cal,' he says.

After a while I stop crying, haul myself up, down the tea and leave the room.

'Cal?' he calls after me.

'I'm going to bed,' I yell back.

'Good idea.' He gets up.

'You can sleep on the sofa.'

'Oh, but Cal…'

'This was all your fault, Micky.'

He doesn't answer because he knows it's the truth. If he thinks for one minute that I don't remember exactly what happened then he is sadly mistaken. Deluded.

I have a night full of nightmares, hardly surprising.

In the morning Micky wakes me with another cup of tea. He's showered and changed his clothes.

'I'll leave it here,' he says, putting the cup on my bedside table. 'I have to go to work.'

'Really?'

'Yeah. It's tricky. You know. Don't want to give them any excuses.'

It's a relief when I hear the front door slam behind him. I listen out for the familiar roar of his car as he starts the engine, the gear changes as he roars up the road.

Why do I feel as though I've done something

wrong? It was him. His fault. Was he so drunk that he can't remember? Even if he'd drunk all those beers it wouldn't affect him like it would me.

I remember every detail.

I don't attempt to get out of bed even though I know I must. I need to shower. I need to make an effort to get better, to recover. Instead I just lie in bed and cry. What else is there to do?

It's lunchtime before I make it downstairs, not that I'm hungry.

He's out there, the builder.

Through the grubby kitchen window I watch him. Feeling my eyes on his back he turns and smiles. Then the smile drops from his face and he looks shocked. I drift away from the window; I don't want to be explaining myself to anyone, least of all a stranger. Tonight I'll tell Micky to stop the extension. What do we need it for now?

I'm sitting on the sofa staring into space; I might have been here an hour or six, I have no idea. There's a knocking coming from somewhere. It stops then starts again. It's insistent.

Eventually I haul myself up. Every part of my body hurts, but no part hurts as much as my heart.

The knocking is on the back door. It's him. The builder.

'So sorry to bother you,' he starts, when I open the door. 'Oh. Oh. What happened?'

'Had an accident,' I lie. I'm not going to tell a complete stranger that my drunken husband knocked me down the stairs and killed our baby.

'What did you want?'

'Just could you fill my water bottle? So sorry.' He holds up an empty plastic squash bottle.

I take it from him, take it to the sink, run the tap, then fill up the bottle.

'Thank you,' he says, when I hand it back. 'Are you all right? Is baby all right?'

I shake my head slowly, my mouth opens, but no sound comes out. It's a silent cry, long and breathless and I feel if I could just pass out, then oblivion could take me.

Before I know what's happening the builder is folding me in his arms. He's bonier the Micky, his body made of sharp edges. But he's warm and secure and I feel oddly safe in the arms of this stranger.

'So sorry,' he mutters.

After a while we move apart. Awkward. Embarrassed. He steps away and I close the door in his face before stumbling back to the sofa.

The builder leaves before Micky comes home. I hear his van start up outside. Maybe his leaving early is deliberate.

'Sorry I'm late, Cal,' Micky says, appearing in front of me.

I just stare at him. I don't care how late he is. I don't care if he never comes home. Why would I?

'Shall I go and get us fish and chips?'

I shake my head. I don't want anything to eat.

'Have you eaten anything today.'

'Doubt it,' I mutter. I can't remember and I don't care.

'You need to eat to get better, Cal.'

'I'm not ill.' I get up and go to the kitchen. I pull a packet of biscuits out of the cupboard, make myself a glass of orange squash and stagger towards the stairs. 'I'm going to bed. On my own.'

His face twists but he doesn't say anything.

I drink the squash in bed but I can't be bothered to open the biscuits. Instead I just slump down the bed and cry myself to sleep.

It's dark when I wake up. The house is silent. There's no echo from the TV downstairs, no splinter of light escaping up the stairs. Either he's asleep or he's gone out.

I go to the toilet, I'm still bleeding a lot. I knew that would be the case after the birth but I didn't mind because it would have been worth it. Not now.

The front door slams.

'Cal,' Micky calls up the stairs.

I can't be bothered to answer him but he's still there in the hallway staring up when I cross the landing on the way back to my bedroom.

'You okay?'

I don't answer. I won't answer. Instead I glance down the stairs, then study each one, wondering which ones my feet knocked against, which ones killed my unborn baby. There's a scuff mark halfway down the wall on one side. Was it there before? The house is such a tip it easily could have been. Or was that me? Or him after he fake threw himself down after me? I study the carpet beneath my feet, old and worn and tatty but not loose. Never loose.

I climb back into bed.

Micky doesn't come upstairs.

Four

It's two weeks and one day since Micky killed our baby.

The pattern of my days, our days, has remained the same. I sleep upstairs, only going down when he's at work. He sleeps downstairs on the sofa, only coming up to use the bathroom and find clean clothes. He must be running out because I haven't done any washing since it happened. But he has. Not clothes as such, but his work uniform. He obviously doesn't iron it, like he made me. I don't cook for him; I don't do anything for him. Why should I? But then, he doesn't do a lot for me.

He did ring work and tell them I wouldn't be in for a while. Of course they wanted a reason and he had to tell them. Then they said they'd need a certificate from my doctor. I rang the surgery myself. I didn't even need to go in, they just sent a *sicknote* through the post to me. I didn't even tell Micky, I just popped it in a new envelope and asked the builder to post it. I need to keep work sweet; I'm going to need that job.

Micky hasn't asked about it. He's too wrapped up in himself. He comes home from work, crashes about in the kitchen and bathroom, though, I notice, he doesn't make any meals, probably because I haven't been shopping. He's lost weight, we both have, me more than him. But I've no doubt he's augmenting his calories with beer every night when he's out with Jez.

Physically I feel much better. The bleeding has almost stopped. Today I'm getting up, I'm getting dressed in proper clothes and I'm stripping the bed and doing some washing.

I'm in the kitchen when Micky comes home. He can't keep the look of shock from his face.

'How are you?' he asks.

'Been better.'

'You look well.' He says this as though he hasn't seen me every day for the last two weeks, albeit briefly. I suppose my being dressed, washing my hair and being upright *is* a shock to him.

'Like I say, I've been better.'

'Something smells nice.' His tone is hopeful.

'I've cooked something from the freezer. Rustled up a meal.' I smile at him, an attempt to appear friendly.

'Cool.'

'Would you like some?'

'I would. Yes, I would.'

'I'll bring it in,' I say, nodding towards the living room where we have a small dining table. We never use it, it's full of post and junk mail; the state of it annoys the hell out of me. We always eat on our laps.

We eat in silence. It's not exactly a gourmet meal, a burger each, some chips and baked beans. Micky usually has two burgers but there weren't enough for that. There weren't any buns either, but I have found a frozen loaf of bread so he has a slice of that too. He doesn't comment and we eat our meal in silence. Afterwards he says thank you and tells me it was good. It's probably the only proper meal he's had since before he slapped me.

'Do you want some pudding?' I ask as I stand up, take his empty plate and head for the kitchen.

'Yes, please.'

It's ice cream from the freezer and fruit from a tin I found at the back of a cupboard. I don't even know when we bought that. Maybe we didn't, maybe it was here when we moved in, left by the previous owner. I don't know and I don't care. I sniffed it and it didn't smell bad, so we're eating it. I need food to build up my strength. I need to make peace with Micky so he doesn't see what's coming. So he doesn't know I'm leaving until I've gone.

I look around the kitchen before I take our pudding through. What a dump. The whole house is a dump. We've done so little since we moved in, a few licks of paint then we stopped because Micky was adamant we should do the extension first. So now we live in a pigsty. This isn't how I thought it would be.

When Mum was alive and it was just me and her, before she became ill, everything seemed so easy, so simple. I was doing well at school. Very well. Predicted grades on my GCSEs were high. Mum and

I had already discussed which A' levels I would do and the school was in agreement. We just had to decide whether I would stay at the same school or go to college. Then it happened, Mum became ill. It went rapidly downhill from there. When I should have been sitting my exams I was arranging her funeral and realising that despite my so-called cleverness, I knew nothing. Mum had tried to prepare me but because her death was sudden she hadn't had enough time.

And now look where I am. I think I preferred my nomadic life of before to this life with Micky.

Would I still think that if my baby boy had lived? And this extension might have been worth the wait and mess, but now it's pointless.

I hand over Micky's pudding bowl and he smiles at me. I nod back. He gobbles down his food like a starving animal. I wonder if he'll tell me he's going out? I decide to pounce before he speaks.

'The extension,' I start, and he frowns in response. 'I think we need to call a halt to it.'

'No way. We've paid up to the roof level.'

'But he's still digging the foundations.' I know this because I watched him for a full five minutes yesterday from the back bedroom window. Eventually, feeling my eyes on his body, he looked up and smiled at me. I stepped away then.

'Yes, I know, but we've paid up to roof level.' He says this as though I hadn't understood it the first time.

'Well get a refund. Stop him now. Pay him for what he's done, or get him to tidy it up a bit. We can spend the money decorating instead. God knows it needs it, especially when we come to sell it.'

He sighs and gives me a look that implies I'm stupid. 'But we're not selling it and we can't get a refund because he's spent most of that money on materials. I explained this to you before.' He sighs again.

'What all of it?'

'Most of it. Anyway he's finishing the footings then awaiting inspection from the council, it's all booked. It's too late to pull out.' His face softens as he looks over at me. 'Anyway, we'll still need the extra space, there will be other babies.' His hand creeps across the sofa towards mine.

I snatch my hand away, grab his empty bowl and stand up.

'What?' he says, as I walk away.

'It's too soon.' What I want to say is that it will never happen because I'm making my escape plan but I can't. I've seen Micky Fisher's true colours and I'm not hanging around for any more of his treatment, however *accidental.*

'Course it is. But you're better now. We'll try again and this time the house will be finished, just how you want it. No dodgy loose carpets.' He smiles at me again. I wonder if he really believes what he's saying or if he just thinks I'm stupid?

'Are you going out?' I hope he is; I can't stand to look at him.

'Yeah. Promised Jez. He's going through a tough time at the moment.'

'Is he?' I wonder if he describes what's happening

to me as a *tough time*?

'Yeah, he's lost his job.'

'He had a job?' I can't keep the shock from my voice. I aways imagined Jez just sat in the pub drinking morning, noon and night. That was certainly my experience when I worked there. I never imagined he had a job.

'Yeah, weekend security guard, but they let him go.' He pauses. 'There was a misunderstanding.'

I don't ask what because I don't care and turn to walk out of the room. But before I go, I remember. 'What about your job? I ask.

'Like you care.' He screws up his face at me but I don't bite. 'Still going on. Been to these meetings, loads of them, consultations they call them.'

'When will you find out?'

'Dunno. They're very secretive. That's the trouble when you don't have a union,' he says, standing up. 'Better get changed if I'm meeting Jez.'

'Yeah.'

I'm just pulling the clean washing out of the washing machine when he appears in the kitchen. He watches me closely for a second or two then speaks.

'I don't suppose there's any of my stuff in there, is there?'

I turn and smile. 'Yes, there is. I'll be putting it in the tumble dryer soon.' I turn back to the washing.

'Cool,' he says. 'I won't be late. Just a swift one with Jez.'

After he's gone I carry the basket through to the room between the living room and the kitchen, the one described as a dining room on the house details when we bought it. It's another dumping ground but it's also where the tumble dryer lives. The plan is to integrate this room into the kitchen and the extension. On paper it looks pretty impressive though it's hard to imagine the reality. I load up the dryer and set it off.

Micky is late coming back, just as I expected, hoped even. I've changed the bedding he's been using and laid out the sofa as his bed again. I've also piled up his fresh, clean clothes.

I hear him groan when he comes in. I smile to myself. If he thinks he's ever sleeping with me again he has another think coming.

In the morning I stay in bed until he's finished his shower and gone back downstairs. Then I sneak across to the bathroom but not before stopping and peering out of the spare bedroom window. The builder is there, he's digging again. I do wonder if this cheapness is worth it. Surely if he had help and a mechanical digger this extension could have been much further on by now. Sensing my presence, he turns and looks up at me, a little smile playing across his face. I step back.

After a shower and dressing, and Micky's departure for work, I go downstairs. Micky has eaten some cereal and left the plate for me to clear up. Mechanically I wash it up, together with his dirty coffee cup. Then I put the kettle on and open the kitchen door.

'Would you like a coffee, or tea?' I ask.

The builder turns and smiles. 'Yes. Please.

Whatever you're having.'

I nod and close the door. That makes life easier. I'll make tea, in a pot. I do like a pot of tea but it's too much for one and Micky prefers coffee.

The sun is shining and it's almost warm when I take a tray with his mug of tea and a plate of biscuits out to him. He turns and smiles as I prop the tray on a pile of blocks.

He glances down at the blocks. 'For the walls,' he says. 'Once the footings go in and pass inspection.'

I nod my agreement. I don't care. Just get on with it. 'Seems like a long old job.'

'Yes. I have to do everything by hand. The alleyway is too narrow to get a digger down here.' He sighs in a theatrical way, then laughs.

'Oh. I thought it was because you were cheap.' That is a cheap shot from me but I can't resist it.

'That too,' he says, laughing, before picking up the tea and taking a swig. 'Good tea. Very good tea.' He knocks back the whole mug.

'Wasn't that hot?'

'Just perfect.'

'Would you like another? There's plenty in the pot.'

'I would.' His smile lights up his face.

When I come back with another mug he's eaten all the biscuits.

'You were hungry.'

'Hungry work.'

'I'd better leave you to it then.'

'Yes. The inspector comes tomorrow. After that I can really get on with the building.'

'Good.'

Micky comes home early. Far too early and when I hear his car roar onto the drive I feel apprehensive. I'm in the kitchen going through the cupboards, checking dates and discarding old stuff. There's plenty of it and I'm pretty sure most of it isn't ours. I'm doing this to stop myself from thinking, to stop myself from sinking back into a well of grief. I'll never get my baby boy back and it's more than I can bear.

'If you can do that you can get back to work,' Micky says, filling the doorway.

I feel sick. He's in foul mood and he's been drinking; I can smell it. I turn and look him in the face but I don't say anything.

'Well?'

'I'm signed off sick for another two weeks.' And I don't want to go back even then. My body may be healing but inside I'm dying.

He grunts. 'Any beer?'

I don't answer. Assuming that he's drunk the beer I bought weeks ago, unless he's bought more, there won't be.

He strides the two steps to the fridge and yanks it open. 'Fuck's sake,' he roars. Then he turns to me. I'm just standing there holding a tin of ancient sardines in my hand. 'Well?' he roars again. 'Aren't you going to ask why I'm home so early? Go on, ask me.'

I can tell by the thunderous look on his face that I have to ask, that I dare not ask.

‘Why are you home so early?’ I keep my voice low, monotone; my attempt not to annoy him further.

‘Been made fucking redundant, haven’t I? The bastards.’

Five

I've never been made redundant myself. Never had a serious job, most have been in bars or shops. Working in the supermarket now is probably the most reliable job I've ever had. Never really had a job long enough for redundancy to be a possibility. But I do know that there's usually a payoff, redundancy money. Micky's worked there for almost twenty years, so there must be something, union or no union.

'I'm sorry,' I tell him, because I am, and not just for him but for myself too.

'Yeah, well, you'll have to get back on those extra shifts asap.' He says asap, as though it's a real word.

I steal myself to ask the question, reminding myself that I do have a right to know; I am his wife. 'You must be getting some sort of payoff?'

He glares at me, then his face is blank and I don't know how he's going to react. Finally, he says, 'Pittance.'

'Oh.' I look down.

'And I won't get it for another two weeks. Fucking nerve of the bastards. Marched me out, us out, there were three of us. The others are bloody ancient, a couple of years off retirement, so they were pleased. I'm still fucking young. I gave them my best bloody years and this is how they treat me. It's because I've been there a long time, worked my way up the pay scale. They didn't get rid of any of the lazy young bastards that stand around all day taking sneaky looks at their phones, because they're cheap. Bastards. Shouldn't be allowed.'

'No.'

Suddenly he stops, then tosses his head towards the window, towards the builder. 'How's he getting on?'

'The inspector's coming tomorrow.'

'And is he ready? Will it pass? Has he done what needs doing?'

I've no idea. I never asked. But I do know I don't want Micky any angrier than he already is. 'Yes, oh yes.'

'That's one fucking good thing. I need a piss.' He turns and stomps off up the stairs. But he's soon back. 'Before you ask,' he starts, glaring at me. 'No, we are not cancelling the extension because of this. You can get your arse back to work and work extra shifts while I look for another job. We need to get this house up to scratch just in case we do have to sell it.'

I'm not going to argue with him, because we *are* going to sell it.

He glares at me again, before turning and flinging open the door to the so-called dining room. He's in there for minutes, cussing and rummaging around before he reappears with a quarter bottle of whisky in his hand. God knows how old that stuff is; there's thick dust on the bottle. Tentatively I open a cupboard door and find him a glass.

'Don't need it.' He unscrews the bottle and puts it to his mouth, taking a big swig and swilling it around.

I fight to keep the distaste from showing on my face. But I'm not as successful as I thought I was.

'Don't look at me like that.' He takes another swig, swallows, then belches. 'I said don't look at me like that, Miss High and Mighty. You think you're so much better than me.'

I shake my head. But he's right, I do. I didn't but I do now. But I've never said it; I've been careful not to.

'I know you think you're too good for me.'

'I don't.'

'Jez has noticed it too.'

Jez. Of course. Jez, who matters so much more to Micky than I do.

'He warned me on our wedding day, said it's not too late to pull out.' He takes another swig then shakes his head. 'He saw through you all right. Saw better than I did. But we are married and you'd better remember that.' He steps towards me; he's still holding the whisky bottle. Is he going to hit me with it?

I step back, feel around on the worktop for the sardine can I put down earlier. He sees my actions and laughs.

'Come here, you silly bint. I'm not going to hurt

you. I love you, don't I?'

The truth is I think he loves me as much as I love him and, at the moment, that's not very much. But he's drunk and with every mouthful he's getting drunker.

With his free hand he reaches over and grabs my arm. 'Put the can down,' he says, grinning.

I lay the sardine can carefully back on the worktop.

'Tell me it's going to be okay. Tell me we're okay. I'm fucking sick of sleeping on that bloody sofa.'

I have to tell him. I have to if I want to keep myself safe. I don't want to *accidently* fall against the worktop and have the whisky bottle hit me around the head.

'We're going to be great, Micky. I'll go back to work soon and you'll easily find another job.'

'That's right. We'll soon be back on track. We'll get this fucking extension done.' He takes another swig of the whisky; it dribbles from the side of his mouth and he cuffs it away and all the time he's still gripping my arm. 'Then we'll have a baby. A proper baby. Planned this time, not an accident.'

I yank my arm away. How dare he say that? He seems to be implying it was my fault, my doing, my duplicity.

'Come here,' he says, raising his voice. 'I want to love you, Cal, but you do make it hard.' Then he laughs before throwing back his head and finishing off the whisky. There may not have been much but he's drunk it all in a matter of minutes. He throws the bottle into the sink where it clatters against the pitted stainless steel. 'Come here.' He reaches for me again but with both arms this time.

He's stronger than me, much bigger too and I can't get away. He's got his hand on my face and he squeezes my jaw as he pushes his mouth over mine. I scream but the sound comes out of my throat, not my mouth because he's enclosed it with his own. The taste of his saliva mixed whisky is nauseating.

I attempt to push him away but that just makes him stronger, his actions more urgent.

'Don't pretend you don't want me, Cal,' he says. 'Because we both know you're hot for it when it suits you.' He can be so vulgar sometimes.

I manage to pull away, put a tiny bit of distance between us, but I'm still trapped between him and the worktop. 'Not yet though, Micky. I'm still healing.'

'You can't use that excuse for ever.' His face takes on a particularly nasty look. 'We're married, remember? And no matter what happens, I'm sleeping in my own bed tonight, with or without you.'

I nod, just once, just so he knows I've heard him. Then he grins.

'It doesn't need to be nasty. Before it happened you loved being with me.'

'*It* happened?' How dare he reduce what happened, what he did to *it*.

'Yeah, the accident.'

'You hit me. That wasn't an accident. You hit me so hard I fell down the stairs and our baby died. That was your fault.'

'Fuck's sake. Can't you let it go. We've got to move on with our lives. Got to move forward and harping on and moping and dwelling on it isn't moving on, is it?' His face is starting to redden with anger.

'It's still early.'

'It's a few weeks, you should be moving on now. Jez thinks you're playing on it.'

'Jez. What the hell does Jez know? I don't give a damn what Jez thinks.'

Micky's face reddens further. I've insulted his best friend, his drinking buddy, but I can't stop myself.

'You think more of Jez that you do of me. He's more important to you than I am, than our baby was.'

'Shut up,' he says. 'Why don't you just keep your damn mouth shut? You've always got to argue. Why I like Jez is because he doesn't bloody argue all the time.'

'Maybe you should have married Jez then.' I know I'm goading him. I know I'm pushing him but I can't stop myself.

When it comes the slap is shocking but not unexpected. Its force knocks me off my feet. I'm scrabbling around on the disgusting kitchen floor with its cracked tiles; I'm trying desperately to get up but my ears are ringing.

'Stay there,' Micky growls.

Before I know what's happening he's down on the floor too, ripping his belt off, tugging at his trouser zip. I skitter backwards across the kitchen to escape him, not that there's anywhere to go. He grabs my left leg and yanks it back to him. I feel a deep pain in my groin and groan. But he's not deterred. He pushes my dress up and out of the way. He's grabbing at my knickers, pulling them while cussing to himself. Finally, they rip on one side and he yanks them out of the way.

He's going to rape me.

My drunken husband is going to rape me.

He doesn't really know what he's doing, does he?

I'm barely healed from the birth of our dead baby and he's going to rape me on our disgusting kitchen floor.

'No, Micky, no,' I cry out. 'Don't do this. Please. You're going to hurt me.'

But it's no good. The Devil is in him now. The Devil and alcohol, and anger at losing his job. And everything is my fault and I must be punished. I can see it all in his face, his crazed eyes, the saliva around his mouth.

His trousers are down around his knees. There is no reasoning with him now.

I wonder how he'll feel when he sobers up? Will he remember what he's done?

He's coming towards me. There is no stopping him now. No reasoning with him. He is beyond reason.

I have to decide now, do I fight him off or do I go limp and hope it won't damage me so much?

I decide on limp.

I wish I still had the sardine can in my hand. I could knock him around the side of his head, maybe knock some sense into him.

I lie there, trying not to brace myself against his onslaught. I must be calm. I must be limp.

He pushes himself inside me and it's hurts so much I scream.

And I scream.

And I scream.

And in his crazed state he puts his hand over my mouth and presses down on my body with his.

I'm crying. Shaking with pain. He's not just raping me, he's brutalising me.

Even with his hand over my mouth I'm still screaming.

Then there's a dull, heavy thud and Micky stops. He flops down heavier on top of me, but at least he's not pushing anymore.

Have I found the sardine can and hit him with it?

Micky's body is heaved off me. Hands reach around my shoulders and gently sit me up. I stare into kind eyes. The builder's eyes. I scrabble to stand up and he helps me, leaning my body against his. He doesn't speak, just blinks. Then he smooths down my dress.

Once upright I gasp for air. I don't know what's going on. The sardine can is still on the worktop. I didn't hit Micky.

Micky is laying on his back, his eyes are closed. There's blood slowly seeping out from underneath his head.

Blood is seeping out from between my legs too, trickling down and dotting onto the floor.

I look at the builder and frown.

'He was hurting you,' he says, as if I need telling.

Then I see it, a claw hammer hanging from his hand. He follows my gaze with his own eyes.

'You. Hit. Him. With. That,' I manage.

'I tried to pull him off. I yelled at him to stop. He wouldn't.'

'No.'

I turn slowly towards the drawer, the one we keep the cutlery in. I pull out a knife, the one we cut bread with, its blade long and serrated, though it's not a bread knife because it has a pointed end. The builder's eyes widen; he thinks I'm coming for him.

Before I know what I'm doing, without even thinking about it, I leap onto Micky and plunge the knife deep into his heart.

Six

I think I can pinpoint the exact moment my life started to go drastically wrong. It was the first time Mum felt a bit *funny*. By funny she meant dizzy and a bit *other-worldly*. She went to bed to sleep it off and the next morning she was back to normal. Obviously just a bit overtired, she thought.

It happened a few more times after that, but in themselves each incident was unremarkable. 'Nothing to worry about,' Mum said. So we didn't worry. What we didn't know then, what we subsequently found out when it was far too late, was that Mum was having a series of mini-strokes. By then Mum had had a major stroke which had left her paralysed, slumped in the chair like a deflated balloon. I came home from school, bounding into the living room to tell her that I'd worked so hard in revision class that even the teacher had congratulated me, to find her like that.

At least she wasn't dead. I called an ambulance and they took us both away. She got a bit better and they let her go home, mainly because she begged to go. I stopped going to school, looking after her was all I cared about. I believed that if I looked after her the very best I could that she would get better. Of course she didn't, she had another stroke instead. But she didn't want to go back to hospital so I looked after her at home for as long as I could and I argued on her behalf with our GP surgery so that they would help a little.

If I could turn back time, if I could go back and force Mum to go and get herself checked out after that first time, or even the second, might things have turned out differently?

I'll never know.

I stare at Micky's bloody, dead body on the grubby kitchen floor. All that blood; it's going to be hard to get it out of the cracks in the tiles.

'Mrs Fisher, Callie.'

Someone is speaking to me. Who?

Oh, him. The builder.

'What?' I snap, then shudder to find I'm clutching the bread knife. The blade is bloody but the handle is not. There are a few splatters of blood on my dress. They could be mine. They could be Micky's.

At least I'm standing up, at least I'm not crouched over his body like a crazy person. I drop the knife on the floor. The builder leans past me and kicks it away. It skitters across the tiles before disappearing under a kitchen unit. That wouldn't have happened if we'd had kickboards. Now someone is going to have to crawl around on the filthy floor and get that out. Me probably.

‘Do you think I should call the police?’ I hear myself say.

‘No.’ Though quiet, his answer it too quick.

‘An ambulance then?’

‘I think it’s too late for that.’

‘But we have to do something. Do you think he’s dead?’ Micky’s once handsome face is contorted into an ugly shape. His eyes, which I’m sure were closed before, are open and staring. It occurs to me that he’ll have a great view of the yellowed and stained ceiling from there. That must have been the last thing he saw.

Or maybe it was my angry face.

‘Did you kill him or did I?’ I ask.

The builder moves towards me and I flinch.

‘Let’s go and sit down,’ he says, laying his hands gently on my shoulders and guiding me into the living room. At least he’s no longer holding the hammer.

Micky’s bedding is piled neatly on one end, *I* did that earlier, so we sit at the other end. Even so I have enough presence of mind to yank at one of the pillows and sit on it, not wanting to stain the sofa with blood, mine or Micky’s. We’re sitting too close together, me and the builder.

‘What have we done?’ I manage before I start wailing.

The builder pulls me into him and I sob on his shoulder for what seems like seconds. Maybe I fall asleep, it’s hard to tell, because suddenly I’m aware that it’s dark outside.

‘We need to call the police.’ It’s the logical thing

to do. It's the right thing to do. I think I killed him. I plunged the knife into his heart. I think it was me. It was self-defence. The fact that he was already unconscious just made it easier. Or was he already dead?

'It is the right thing to do,' the builder says. 'But I must leave first.'

'No, you can't do that. You're my witness. You saw him attacking me. You pulled him off.'

'I didn't pull him off. I couldn't. I hit him with a hammer.'

'To protect me. What I did was self-defence.'

'Was it? He was already off you when you stuck the knife in his chest.'

He's right, I know he is. Micky was no longer a danger to me when I did that. Not at that time anyway. That was the point when I should have called an ambulance.

'You call the police. I must go now.'

'But you can't. Anyway, they'll come and find you.'

'They won't find me.' He stands up. 'Perhaps if I hadn't hit him it would have been better.'

'No, no, he was hurting me. Badly. Why must you go? Why can't you stay? We can say that he started to get up again, that's why I stabbed him.'

'Why *did* you stab him? He was already down.'

'I don't know. I didn't think about it. It just happened.' I wanted to punish him.

'I'll go now.' He turns to walk away. 'Give me five minutes to collect my tools. I will need them.'

'But you can't. They'll find you anyway. It will

look better for you, for me, if you stay.'

'I can't stay.' He leaves, trudging out past Micky's body and out into the dark garden.

I look around for my phone, trying to remember where I left it, when I had it last. Is it upstairs? Is it in the kitchen? I steal myself to go into the kitchen. The builder is covering Micky's body with a piece of black plastic.

'Is he definitely dead?' I ask, suddenly thinking he might not be and we've wasted this time when we should have called an ambulance.

'Long dead,' he says. 'I think *I* killed him.'

'No, I did. His eyes were closed before I stabbed him. I think.'

'I must go. Have you rung the police now?'

'No, I don't know where my phone is.'

He nods slowly then points over into the corner of the worktop. There it is, sitting right next to the sardine can. I look at it but I don't pick it up.

'What's your name?'

He almost laughs, a little snort escaping through his nose.

'Mick,' he says.

'Oh yes, of course. How could I have forgotten that? Short for Michael, same as Micky.'

'No, short for Mikhail.'

'I thought I detected a foreign accent there. Faint but definitely there.' I marvel at how I'm able to say something so ordinary while standing over Micky's dead body.

'Yes, that's why I have to go.' He turns away towards the garden and his tools. 'I'm sorry, I won't be able to finish your building work.'

'I never wanted it anyway,' I say, again without much thought.

He shrugs.

'Hey, what if I don't call the police?'

He glances down at the plastic covering Micky then looks back at me.

'Won't he be missed? At work? By his family? You have no choice but I must go.'

'Why? Why must you go? Why can't you stay and help me out?'

He looks at me for a long, long time. It could even be minutes. I don't push him, I don't speak. I can almost see him thinking, his face showing the processing of thoughts. He's clean shaven and has dark, expressive eyes. Kind eyes. Despite what's happened. What he's done. What I've done.

'I'm illegal. They'll deport me.'

I let out a long snorting laugh. 'We're probably both going to go to prison for a very long time and you're worrying about being deported.'

'You wouldn't understand.' He turns away again, his hand on the kitchen door.

'Wait. Wait. No one will miss him. He lost his job today. He doesn't see his family.' I pause as he stands still, frozen in thought. 'Ever,' I add. 'I've never met any of them.'

He nods but he doesn't say anything.

'So, what if I didn't call the police?'

'Why did you stab him?'

He's been honest, I should be.

'He killed my baby. He hit me and I fell down the

stairs. It was his fault. Entirely.'

His mouth forms into a silent 'O'.

'So, what if I didn't call the police?' I can hardly believe I'm even considering an alternative, but I am.

He looks at me, looks away, sighs. Those expressive brown eyes look sad.

'Bury him.'

I nod. 'Where?' Under the patio? We don't have a patio. And everyone knows that bodies under patios always get found.

'In the footings.'

'Aren't they being inspected tomorrow?'

'Yes. I can dig deeper, hide him. Once they've passed inspection I will be filling with concrete.'

I turn away, go back to the living room and drop onto the pillow on the sofa. He appears in the doorway.

'You've really thought this through,' I say.

'I had time while you slept. He was a cruel man. He hurt you.'

'You didn't know that then.'

'I did. I saw how he looked at you. I saw that he left you alone when you were ill.'

'He had to go to work,' I interrupt.

He lifts his eyes up to mine and then drops them. 'I heard how he spoke to you.' This time he looks me in the eye. 'I heard how he spoke about you.'

'What? What do you mean?'

The builder gives a little shake of his head then leaves the room. Seconds later he's back with my phone. 'Ring the police,' he says, handing me the phone. I sit and stare at it.

'What did he say about me? Who to?'

'It doesn't matter. Ring the police. Then I'll leave.' He watches me, waiting. 'Unless you really need me to stay.'

'But then what will happen to you?'

He shrugs. 'It doesn't matter. Between us we killed a man. A cruel man. A man who beat you. But we still killed him. I'll back up whatever you want to say. I'll tell them that he got up and started to attack you again.'

I stare at my phone. I type in my password and pull up the dialler. It's just three little numbers: 999. So easy. After that I'll just be answering questions.

Endless questions.

I let the phone go off again, while I'm still staring at it.

'Where are your family?' I ask him.

'All gone. I was the only one to survive, to escape.'

'Where from?'

He doesn't answer immediately but when he does, he looks away. 'Syria,' he whispers.

I drop the phone on the sofa. 'Sit down.'

He hesitates then complies.

'They won't send you back to Syria.'

'And you know this?'

We sit for a long while in silence. I don't know what to do. In one way Micky's death, however horrible the circumstances, is a relief. No more of his drinking, no more fear of his violence – whether real or accidental. No more bad temper.

But I killed him. He may have been raping me,

but I killed him. It wasn't really self-defence. Not really. I don't think it was murder. Manslaughter perhaps. Would the sentence be less for that? I've read in the papers about coercive control. Was Micky doing that to me? Would my losing our baby after an *accident* be a mitigating circumstance? Would anyone believe me?

Micky only hit me that once.

But he did kill my baby boy.

Seven

'How long will it take?'

The builder looks at me and frowns.

'To bury him.' I can hardly believe what I'm asking.

'I'll need to dig one of the trenches deeper, a lot deeper.'

'Judging by how long it's taken you to do what you have it might be days.' That was mean but truthful.

He shrugs.

'Two hours perhaps.'

'It's dark out there. Won't you need lights?'

'The kitchen light will do. We hardly want spotlight on what we're doing.'

'No. We don't.' Are we really going to do this? Am I going to do this? 'What do I need to do?'

'You stay in here. I'll dig. You might have to help me move the body.'

So Micky is *the body* now. Not Micky any longer.

'Do you want me to dig or are you ringing the police?' He grabs my phone from the table where I dropped it earlier and hands it to me.

I take the phone and put it back on the table. 'Dig,' I mutter.

He's out there for an hour before I venture out into the kitchen. Micky is still there, covered in black plastic. I look down on him and feel nothing. It's weird. I should be freaking out, I should be hysterical, but I'm not, not now anyway.

I open the back door.

'Nearly done,' he says.

'Why does it take so long?'

'Your ground is hard, lots of rocks and stones. You will have to help me move…' he hesitates, 'him.'

'Okay. Let me know when.'

I turn back to the kitchen, close the door behind me. I reach for the kettle and hold it under the tap, then I realise how wrong that would be. I can't be making cups of tea with Micky dead on the floor. I dump the kettle and wander back to the sofa.

'Okay,' a voice says.

I jump. For a minute I think it's Micky. I must have dozed off.

'Are you okay to help?' Mik the builder asks.

'Yes.' I haul myself up, attempt to shake off my sleepiness. It seems so wrong to be tired when I've murdered my husband.

In the kitchen Mik has wrapped more black plastic around Micky. He's tied it up so I can't see anything of Micky's body. He's mopped up a lot of the blood too. I don't know what he's used. I could almost believe that nothing ever happened.

Until we pick him up. He's heavy. Strong as Mik the builder must be I don't think he could do this alone. Between us we drag him to the door but then we have to lift him over the threshold. His head clonks down on the ground outside. Poor Micky, that must have hurt. Then we alternately lift and drag him to the ditch. It isn't far, maybe eight feet but it's hard going. Or maybe we're just weak. We line him up parallel with the ditch.

'You don't have to stay for this part, I can manage alone now.'

'I should stay. I must stay.'

He shrugs, then leans down and rolls Micky into the ditch. It's deep and when he hits the bottom there's a sort of plop sound and a splash of water.

'Below the water table,' Mik says. 'Do you want to say some words?'

Like a funeral, he means. I lean over and look at the plastic at the bottom of the trench. 'Sorry,' I whisper, before turning around and going back inside, leaving him to fill the ditch again.

In the morning it's raining.

'Will it wash all the earth away?' I ask, turning to Mik the builder who is dozing on his end of the sofa. I've moved to the other end, wrapped Micky's bedding around me.

'Wouldn't think so. What time is it?'

'I don't know.'

'I need to check. The inspector could come any time after eight.' He gets up and trudges outside. 'It's fine,' he says when he comes back in.

I get up. I have a headache. Not surprising really.

'Tea? Coffee?' I ask him.

'Whatever you're having,' he says, his voice quiet.

I go through the motions in the kitchen, make a pot of tea while he waits in the living room. Last night I cleaned the floor again, mopped it with bleach. He'd used the old mop that was here when we moved in to soak up the blood, Micky's blood, so I had to bleach it, and the floor, clean. The smell of bleach still lingers.

'I don't suppose you have anything to eat?' he asks from the door.

'Yes, sorry. I expect you are hungry. You've worked hard.' That sounds so wrong on so many levels because it is wrong, of course it is. 'Toast?' I ask.

He nods and I pop two slices into the toaster, both for him because I don't think I'll be eating again, ever.

He has two more slices after the first two. Seems fair, he has a lot more work to do today.

He uses the bathroom then goes outside, starts hauling things about and looking busy. I'm still wearing the blood-splattered dress, the rape dress. I won't be wearing it again. Ever.

Mik the builder is wearing some of Micky's old clothes. His own were filthy after the deep digging and it was him who initially cleaned the blood off the kitchen floor. He even retrieved the bread knife from under the cupboards and washed it up. He stuffed his own clothes in a big bag, says we need to burn them, and my dress, says he'll do it in the garden. It won't be today now, not with the rain.

He looks okay in Micky's clothes. They're a little bit loose but perfectly wearable and it's not as if Micky is going to need them again; he said he was saving them for decorating but he won't be doing that now. I feel sad for a moment, but oddly, it quickly passes. Then I get in the shower and cry. I don't think Micky deserved to die, not really. But what's done is done and can't be undone. And he was raping me. And he did kill our baby. So maybe he did deserve it.

Downstairs, I add my dress to the bin bag of Mik's clothes; it's in the so-called dining room. Then I fetch the blood-stained pillow I sat on, Micky's pillow and add that to the bag.

Mik knocks on the kitchen door which seems strangely formal after last night. I open it.

'Mrs Fisher, this is the building inspector. He's passed the footings.' Mik grins.

'Morning,' I manage. 'Thank you.'

The man nods then tells Mik that he'll be back for the next stage and just to let him know via email when he's ready.

I make us both another cup of tea then wander back into the living room, put the TV on and fall asleep. When I awake there's a horrible grinding sound going on, churning and churning and very irritating. It isn't helping my headache. Then it stops and Mik appears in the living room doorway.

'It's done. Concrete just has to set now.'

'What was that noise?'

'Mixer,' he says. 'I was cleaning it out. I can't really

do anything else now, until it sets. I'm going to go home now.'

'But then I'll be on my own…'

He looks at me for a long while, his eyes flitting around the room, momentarily resting on my face. 'Do you want me to stay?'

'No, you'd better go. People will be missing you. What about your family?'

'No family,' he says.

'You should go. It looks odd. Someone will notice you being here all the time. One of the neighbours maybe. When will you be back?'

'Monday. The concrete should have gone off by then. Then I can start on block course. It's stopped raining but I've covered everything just in case it starts again.'

'Okay.' I stand up. I feel I want to thank him formally; I'm fighting the urge to shake his hand. It's so ridiculous.

'If it's dry on Monday we'll have that bonfire.' He turns to leave.

'Won't that look odd?'

'No. Normal. I've already had a couple while I've been here. Your rotten timbers burnt really well and I'll have a few more so it won't just be our clothes.'

I nod and he leaves. After he's gone I stand at the front window and watch him walk down the drive, past Micky's car and out to his van parked on the street. It's navy and smart for a builder and fairly new too. There's no writing on it, no advertising his building firm. It sets me wondering but I suppose if he's illegal he won't want to draw attention to himself.

The weekend is the longest one of my life. I alternate between sleeping and crying. I'm riddled with guilt, of course I am. Is it too late to call the police, to confess? Twice I've picked up my phone, dialled the first two numbers then stopped myself. What would it achieve? Confessing isn't going to bring Micky back. My going to prison won't resurrect him. He did rape me; he did kill our baby. I go through this same argument in my head over and over again, looping on and on. Whatever I decide to do now won't change a thing.

Micky is never coming back.

On Sunday I decide to clear out the dining room, the dumping room. I'm doing it to distract myself, to attempt to stop the guilt-justification loop. It doesn't really work but at least the room is a lot tidier by the end of the day. There's a sizeable pile that can be burned along with the evidence. If we're having a bonfire it might as well be worthwhile.

When Mik arrives on Monday morning he looks fresh and rested.

'How are you?' he asks.

'Been better.'

'Me too.'

'Really, I was just thinking how well you look.'

He shakes his head slowly. 'I stood in the shower for twenty minutes this morning trying to wash the guilt away. My housemate was banging on the door telling me to hurry up.'

'Your housemate,' I echo.

‘I live in a shared house. It’s not particularly nice but it’s cheap and the landlord doesn’t ask any questions as long as I pay cash.’

I nod. It seems to me that Mik the builder inhabits a world of cash. It sounds dodgy.

But not as dodgy as murder. Manslaughter, I correct myself.

‘How long have you lived there?’

‘Just six months, since my uncle’s house was sold.’ He looks wistful. ‘I need to get on. The blocks and bricks are arriving soon. Need to deal with them. Need to build.’

I ask him when we’re having the bonfire, explaining that I have a lot more stuff to burn and he tells me mid to late afternoon, no sooner.

‘Have you eaten much?’ he asks.

I shake my head. How can I eat anything? ‘Not a lot of food in the house.’

‘Maybe you should go and buy some. You need to eat. If you’re going to get through this, you need to look after yourself.’

I nod my agreement. It seems like the strangest thing ever, worrying about what I’m eating, if I’m eating, when Micky’s body is lying out there under tonnes of concrete.

There’s a loud rapping on the kitchen door and it makes me jump.

‘Don’t worry, that’s the delivery.’ He heads outside and I can soon hear voices and everything sounds normal.

Almost comforting.

Eight

I need to get some groceries. I've not been too bothered about food but today, Tuesday, I ran out of milk. Since tea is my staple diet at the moment and I cannot drink it black, I need to venture out.

I don't want to. I should have asked Mik the builder to get some milk, he's part of the reason why I don't have any because I keep feeding him tea too.

I'm upstairs and I take the opportunity to spy on him while he works. He's putting the blocks up with speed and accuracy, certainly more speed that he managed when he demolished the old building and dug the footings. I shudder at the thought of those trenches.

Poor Micky.

Is it too late to call the police? I imagine the walls which Mik has so carefully built being demolished, the concrete broken down. How will they do that? The trench being excavated. Micky's body being brought up, wrapped in plastic, covered in blood.

Mik turns and looks up at me, a tiny little smile plays across his face. I step back and let the curtain drop. I don't smile back. What is there to smile about?

I need to go out. I must shop. I really don't want to.

In the kitchen I look through the cupboards, there's so very little in them, ditto the fridge. There's more in the freezer though, I could survive on that. But I don't freeze milk.

I can't go to the supermarket I work in. I can't let people I know see me yet. The other big supermarket – and it must be a big one because I need the anonymity of masses of people – is five miles across to the other side of town.

I'll need to take the car, Micky's car. The one he only lets me drive when it suits him, infrequently. I don't even have my own set of keys for the car. I told him once that that was weird, married couples always had their own set of keys for the family car. He told me there was only one key, always had only been ever since he bought it and he certainly wasn't going to waste a fortune paying for another one just for me to use it occasionally. He said we had better things to spend our money on.

Like this extension. What's going to happen when the money runs out, when it reaches the point that's been paid for? Can I sell the house with a half-built extension? Can I sell the house with Micky's body in the foundations?

I make a shopping list; it has bread and milk and cheese on it. I can't think of anything else. Maybe I'll be inspired once I get inside the supermarket, see what there is to tempt me. I really don't want to go out. I go back upstairs and arrange my hair into something tidy, then after seeing how thin and pale I look I slap on a bit of CC cream, and a slick of lip gloss. I used to wear makeup all the time before I met Micky and when we were first together, but lately I just haven't had the energy to bother. Or the inclination.

I go downstairs and take another look through the cupboards – I don't know why because I'm looking but not seeing. I open the back door.

'I'm going to the shops,' I say to Mik. 'Do you want anything?' I shudder as I hear myself speak. 'Those are the exact words I used to use to Micky, but that was long ago before I worked in the supermarket and got everything and lugged it home no matter what.

He shakes his head.

'How's it going?' I should show some interest in his building, this extension to my house.

'Good, really good. This is the good bit where you see progress, unlike the groundwork…' It's then that he realises what he's said and stops speaking.

I just stare at him. Then I step back, close the door and go inside. I need to find Micky's car keys.

That's when it hits me. I feel sick and double over in a panic. Gasping for breath I yank the door open again. Mik looks up at me and frowns.

'Are you okay?'

That's almost laughable, of course I'm not okay. 'Come in, come in.' This isn't a conversation I want to have outside. Even though our – my – neighbours' houses aren't especially close but you never know how sound might travel.

'I think we buried Micky's keys. And probably his phone.'

'Are you sure?'

'No. But he always keeps them both in his pocket.'

'His trouser pocket?'

'I think so.' I can't think straight.

'Don't you have a spare?'

'No. I don't.' And I definitely don't want to get into that. I grab my phone and ring Micky's phone. We stand in silence waiting to hear it ring in the house. Praying for it. But nothing. I keep it ringing and open the back door. There's no sound out there either.

'Do you think we'd hear it?' I ask him.

He shrugs. I can tell by his face he's thinking the same as me, that it's the best part of six feet under and covered in concrete, earth, bricks and blocks.

'Wouldn't battery be flat by now anyway?'

'I suppose,' I say, closing the door. 'What am I going to do? I can't leave his car there and never move it again, can I?'

'Are you sure his keys and phone aren't in the house?'

'I don't know. I don't know anything anymore.'

'Was he wearing a jacket?'

'He had his fleece on when he went to work, I think.'

'He wasn't wearing his fleece when we…' his voice fades away. 'Where's his fleece? What colour is it?'

'Black.'

'Okay where would he leave it?'

I've never thought about where Micky discards his clothes. The place is such a tip that anything added or taken away doesn't make much difference.

'What about in there?' Mik nods towards the dining room.

'No, I tidied up in there, I would have noticed it.'

'Okay, let's look around, let's check every inch, let's see if we can find it, because it must be here, somewhere.' He scans the kitchen which is so small that anything as large as a man's fleece jacket would stand out like a sore thumb.

'It's hardly in here,' I sneer.

'Just checking.'

We go through to the living room, look around, I lift up the blankets still there from Micky's makeshift bed, I check the floor behind the sofa, I even look behind the TV.

'This it?' Mik holds up a grey sweatshirt. It's definitely Micky's but not one I've seen him wear lately.

'No,' I say, taking it. 'Where was it?'

'Stuffed behind this pillow.' He stabs at the cushion on the armchair.

'Cushion,' I correct.

'Cushion. Yes. That's a good sweatshirt. I like the logo.'

I inspect the sweatshirt myself. I bought it for him for our first Christmas together. The logo, as Mik has called it, is actually a large graphic of a fish.

'You may as well have it,' I say. 'Keep you warm

while you're working.' I toss it to him.

He raises his eyebrows at me.

'Have it. I have no use for it. Neither does Micky now.' There's only a little waver in my voice. He's returned the clothes he borrowed but he might as well have kept them too. 'Please have it,' I add.

'Thank you, Callie,' he says, his accent evident when he says my name, as it is every time.

I shrug. I'm stopping myself from remembering the last time Micky wore it – I genuinely don't remember – and I don't want to.

Happier times.

'It could be in his car?'

'It might be, but his keys won't be. Are you sure he wasn't wearing it when, you know…?

He shakes his head, then pulls Micky's grey sweatshirt over his head, goes outside to retrieve his baseball hat and stands in the doorway waiting for me to comment. I don't. I can't. A quick glance and he could be Micky.

'I check the car?' he says.

'Okay.'

I watch from the front door as he tries all the doors, which, of course are locked. He looks in every window then turns and comes back inside.

'The fleece is in the car. And I can see his phone in the pocket, it's hanging out.'

'So we're just looking for the keys now then.' Which is doubly annoying because the fleece would have been easier to spot.

Mik insists that we move the furniture to check underneath. I stand back and let him do it, he's strong, I'm not. I've only just recovered from giving birth and being raped, I can't risk lugging heavy stuff around.

'I bet they're in his pocket.' I feel as though I'm stating the obvious. The blindingly obvious.

Mik looks at me and shakes his head slowly. 'No,' he says.

'How do you know?'

'Come with me.'

We go out to the kitchen and he opens a bottom drawer, it's the one where we keep all the junk, the batteries, the pens that don't work, a couple of screwdrivers. I never go in it. He pulls out Micky's wallet.

'You emptied his pockets?'

'Yes.'

I feel sick at the thought of it. Yet, compared to hitting him over the head, stabbing him, and burying him under tonnes of concrete it's minor really.

'You didn't say before.'

'I hoped not to upset you.'

'No. Okay.'

'No keys,' he says, handing me the wallet.

I sigh before going back into the living room, flopping down on the sofa, which isn't in exactly the same spot it was before, and putting my head in my hands. They have to be here somewhere. What does he normally do with them when he walks in. Where does he put them when he's not just lost his job? I can't think straight. Is it any wonder? I play the events of that day, which already seems a long time ago and yet less than a week has passed. I was in the kitchen; he was behind me. I don't recall the keys in his hand then.

'He can't have locked them in the car, can he?' I'm thinking out loud.

Mik, who has stayed in the kitchen, comes into the living room, a tiny smile on his face. He hands Micky's keys over.

'Where?'

'Under the kitchen units.'

'Be better when we get new ones with kickboards,' I say, before slamming my hand over my mouth. I can't believe I've just said that.

Nine

Finding Micky's keys produced another problem. Probably more serious.

After I'd got into the car I picked up his phone from the front seat. The battery was flat after all these days and I didn't give it much thought as I popped it into my handbag before I went into the supermarket.

I don't know what was going on in my head but as well as the milk and bread I desperately needed I also bought enough groceries to make a meal, a special meal.

And not just for me.

When I got home, happy that I hadn't seen anyone I know while I was shopping, I told Mik that when he'd finished for the day he should stay and eat with me.

I'd even bought a bottle of wine. What the hell is going on in my head? I really don't know. I've even cleared the dining table in the living room, getting rid of most of its contents into the bin. There are only so many flyers for pizza delivery that a person needs, I don't know why Micky always insisted on keeping them, though the odd one does have a money off voucher. I can't remember us ever ordering a pizza. Maybe he bought them with Jez.

'I don't really drink alcohol,' Mik says, when I put the bottle and the glasses on the table.

'Oh, sorry. I never even thought. Is it a religious thing?' I go to swipe the bottle away.

'No,' he says, placing his hand on mine. 'Not at all, just don't like the taste or the effect. But don't let me stop you. Let me pour.'

I feel embarrassed now, but if I refuse it'll just make it more awkward. 'I'll just get the food,' I say, scuttling out to the kitchen.

Before I sit down to eat I remember Micky's phone which is still in my handbag, quickly I fish it out and plug the charger in. Fortunately, Micky keeps his phone charger permanently plugged into the socket by the sofa. I don't really know why I'm charging it; it's not as if Micky will be looking at it, yet there might be something of interest. It occurred to me when I was wandering around the supermarket and when I used my debit card to pay for the shopping, that I don't have a clue how our finances work. My wages went into the joint account, as did Micky's, and I think he paid for everything from that account. I've never even seen a bank statement, or a utilities bill come to that. If I'm going to survive without Micky – and it seems I've made the decision that I am, that I must – then I need to understand these things. I'm annoyed with myself for letting Micky take away my independence.

I may not have had much money before I met him, but I knew where it was. I suppose I just liked being looked after.

'It's kind of you to cook for me,' Mik says, eating his meal as though it's the first meal he's had in weeks. Maybe it is.

'Least I could do.' I let the words hang in the air, because really they are so stupidly inappropriate. What am I thanking him for? Disposing of my husband's body after I'd murdered him? I push my food away at this thought, suddenly I've completely lost my appetite, though it had only slightly returned anyway.

Mik eyes my half-full plate. 'Are you going to eat that?' He nods at the chicken, vegetables and sauté potatoes.

'No, I'm full.'

He nods slowly but doesn't take his eyes from my leftovers.

'Would you like it?' I can't believe he wants to eat off my plate.

He hesitates for a moment before speaking, 'If you don't want it. Shame to waste good food.'

Maybe it was like that where he originally came from, little food. Maybe that's why he can't bear to see me wasting it. Up close he's quite gaunt looking. Was he like that before we murdered Micky or, like me, has he lost his appetite since?

'Please, help yourself.' I watch as he swoops on my plate. It doesn't take him long to eat it, while I finish my wine and refill my glass. I need to be careful, this stuff is going straight to my head, especially without a stomach full of food to soak it up. 'So what do you normally do for dinner?' I ask him.

He finishes my leftovers and smiles. 'Whatever I can get,' he says. 'McDonald's, some fish and chips, or pizza. Whatever's cheapest, on offer.'

'Takeaway? Don't you cook for yourself?'

'Beans, maybe, rice sometimes. Don't really have a proper kitchen.'

'I thought you lived with other people.' Now I'm confused.

'Just one room each. A shared bathroom. No kitchen. No living spaces.'

'Oh. I see. It sounds as grim as this.'

'This is good compared to where I live. Once the building work is done here, this will be very good.'

'Yes, well I can't really afford it.' I wince as I say the words.

'I ordered the roof trusses today.'

'I thought we only paid to roof level. I didn't realise they were included.'

He smiles briefly then stands up, picks up the plates and takes them out to the kitchen. I follow him but I don't press him for an explanation about the roof trusses because I really don't want to have to think about it. Thinking too much is painful. For today, this evening, I'm just going to enjoy a pleasant, civilised meal. It's the first one I've had in a very long time.

'There's pudding,' I say. 'It's only shop bought apple pie but there's also cream to go with it.'

'Sounds amazing, Callie,' he says, his accent just

audible on my name again.

'Well, it'll be filling if nothing else. You go and sit down.'

We eat pudding together, even I do, finding the sweetness easier to stomach than the savoury. Afterwards he helps me clear up, even standing at the ancient, disgusting metal sink and washing up, insisting that *he* does it as I cooked for *him*.

I don't think Micky ever washed up. Even when I was ill in bed I think he just ate at work or didn't much bother. Or maybe used the pizza coupons. If he did he never offered me any pizza.

'I'd better be going,' he says, once the kitchen is cleared.

I'm tempted to ask him to stay for the evening, but how odd would that look? As odd as it is.

After Mik's gone I check Micky's phone to see how charged it is. Barely thirty-percent but I switch it on anyway, I'll just have to sit with the power cable in.

The good thing about Micky is that he has no time for unnecessary passwords, so his phone isn't locked. The bad thing about Micky is that he seems to spend a lot of time exchanging messages with Jez. There are twenty-two unanswered messages from him. They are variations of the same four questions:

Where are you?

Thought we were meeting tonight?

Are you ill?

Is your phone broken or lost? What an idiot; if either were the case he'd hardly answer, would he? Jez's brain is obviously addled by all the alcohol he consumes.

The last message, sent about an hour ago, is different. It's not actually a threat, or rather, it wouldn't be to Micky, but to me it's very worrying.

Where the hell are you? Are you dead? I'm going to have to come round to your house if you don't answer.

The last thing I want is Jez on my doorstep.

I flick through the messaging history examining their conversations, checking how Micky usually replies. There are messages referring to me, many in an unflattering way, especially how fat I've become while pregnant. Recently he's complained a lot about my being ill, what a nuisance it is. I catch my breath, tears springing into my eyes. He obviously didn't give a damn about me, or our dead baby. I compose myself; I have to reply to Jez. I ignore the criticism of me and read on. It's soon obvious that Jez is quite needy and demanding and Micky is often short with him.

Was, I correct myself. Was.

I compose a message which I hope covers all Jez's questions and stops any idea of him coming round in person.

Hi, sorry. Phone battery wouldn't charge so had to get another. Lost my job so licking my wounds. And Cal's ill again – getting sick of that too. Think I've caught it so don't come round. M. I press send and hope for the best, imagining my message winging its way to Jez's phone and wondering what his reaction will be. I don't have to wait long to find out.

That's shit mate. Let me know when you're ok.

I let out a long sigh of relief. I've bought some

time but I don't know how much. I really didn't factor Jez into my thinking when I said no one would miss Micky. That was remiss of me, naive and stupid.

I scan through the rest of Micky's messages, there aren't many conversations. Just Jez – primary and most used; me, usually quick stuff about being late and the odd one from the bank confirming when he's set up new payees. I shudder, because banking is something I need to sort out and I have no idea how.

I flick through the rest of the apps on Micky's phone. He doesn't do *Facebook* or any of the other social media platforms. I do. I like looking at other people's lovely lives on *Instagram*, but I never post anything, never even comment. I find his email app and fortunately the phone logs straight into his account. I scan through his emails. Most are junk, offers of loans, discounts for things he'd never buy, but buried in amongst these I find one from his work, it arrived the day he finished – the day he died. It's already been opened.

I choke with shock as I read it. Micky told me that he wasn't getting much in the way of redundancy money. But he lied. It would take me five years to earn this amount of money.

It seems I can afford the extension.

Then what? Stay here and enjoy it? With Micky's body under my feet. Sell and risk someone else finding Micky's body?

I don't think I'm going to be sleeping very well tonight.

Yet oddly, I do. It must the comfort blanket of all that money. I wake with the dawn and face a whole set of questions which have obviously been going around and around in my head while I've slept. Why did he not tell me the truth? Why did he hide how much they were going to pay him? Was he planning on dumping me and keeping it all for himself? Or was he planning on staying with me and keeping it all for himself? Was he going to spend it all on drinking with Jez? And that's another issue, what am I going to do about Jez?

But the biggest question that is looping inside my head is how the hell am I going to get my hands on it? Because it'll go straight into his, no our, now *my* bank account and other than via debit card or cash machine I cannot get at it. I don't have access to it. I suppose I could go to the bank – if I can find a branch that's still open for business – and ask them about it. But wouldn't that look odd? Wouldn't they ask where my husband is? Wouldn't they say he can move it anywhere via his banking app?

Then, sitting up in bed I start to cry. Not for the money. Well, not completely for the money, but for what I've done to Micky. I've killed him. I've buried him.

I am a bad person.

So, to some extent was Micky.

On the plus side, if I can get my hands on that money, the extension can be finished before I have to decide what I'm going to do next.

Ten

Mik is already busily working when I come down for breakfast – a giant mug of coffee with lots of sugar. I make him one too.

'Come inside and drink it,' I tell him, leaving it on the kitchen worktop. Once he's in I let him take a few sips and help himself to the biscuits I bought on yesterday's shopping trip before I speak. 'Is there much more to buy to finish the extension?'

'Yes. The roof tiles, the felt…' he reels off a long list the contents of which completely pass me by. Evidently, I don't have the brain capacity to pay attention to such detail. I wonder if that is baby brain or murder brain? Probably a combination of both.

'What?' I ask, staring into his face as he waits for me to speak. 'Sorry, you lost me there, that's a long list.'

'It is.'

'And all those things have to be paid for?'

'Yes, some are ordered but it's cash before delivery.'

'Could I pay with my debit card?'

He looks alarmed. 'Not to me.'

'Why not?'

'No facility for debit card.' The way he says this sounds very stilted. But he's a small business, a one-man band, so I understand that.

'What about to the suppliers?'

He winces.

'Well how do you usually pay your suppliers?'

'Cash only now.'

'So Micky gave you cash?'

He nods slowly.

'The problem,' I start then stall before continuing. 'Is that there may be money to continue but I can't get at it other than by debit card. And there's a limit on how much I can draw out from cash machines each day.'

'Your husband drew money out over several days.' He looks at me before he continues, 'Why can't you get at your money?'

I sigh a little. 'Micky controlled our finances. I was never involved.'

'But you have joint account?' There's his accent again, and a missing word.

'Yes, but I don't know how to access it.'

'Is app on Micky's phone?'

'Yes, but I can't open it.'

'If you have joint account you should be able to set up online banking for yourself.'

'I should, shouldn't I? But I don't have all the information, not even the account number. My debit card is one of those blank ones to prevent fraud.' I'm tired now, sick of thinking about it. 'Okay, I'll see if I can get cash.'

'Would you like me to look at the app on your husband's phone?'

Do I? Do I trust him? We're a pair of murderers and worse than that we've disposed of a body, my husband's body. Who is the worst of us? Him or me? Because, and this realisation has crept up on me, I feel very little remorse for Micky's death.

'Just had another thought,' I tell him, feeling as though a lightbulb has come on in my brain. 'I can look at the account balance and transactions at a cashpoint machine. I can transfer money to your account that way.' I almost punch the air at my brilliance.

He watches me for a little while before shaking his head. 'No.'

'No? Why not?'

'I don't have bank account.'

'Of course you do.' I laugh at his joke.

'No. Remember, I told you I am illegal. I have no status here. No bank account, no passport. I am a non-person. Why do you think I'm so cheap? Why cash only?'

I don't know whether he's looking for sympathy but I can't summon any up.

'Okay, well at least I can check the balance and get to the cash. I hope I have enough,' I mutter, because it's just occurred to me that maybe the reason why Micky said he was getting very little was because he owes money to the bank, has a loan or an overdraft and his pay out will be needed to pay it all back. Or maybe as well as being a drinker he was a gambler too. So many scenarios go through my head it spins.

Mik goes back outside while I wash up our coffee mugs before sloping off to the living room to work out what I can do next.

I click on Micky's phone and pull up the banking app. It's asking for specific characters from his password. I don't have a clue. It could be anything. I try my name – you never know – but it doesn't work. I try Micky's name and that doesn't work either and now the app is telling me I only have one more try before it locks me out. I drop the phone as though it's burning me. Then I pick it up again, because I think I saw something which might help. At the bottom of the screen is a line that asks *Forgotten your log in details?* I click on it.

It's asking for Micky's email address. I have to click on the email app to find his address because I've never emailed him so have no idea. It takes me several seconds to find it, then I go back to the banking app and type it in. A message pops up saying an email has been sent to me, or rather Micky.

I click back but there's nothing there. Damn, did I put the right address in? Dare I have another go or is there a limit? I put the phone down on the coffee table and decide I'll have to go to a cashpoint machine. I'm about to get up when the phone flashes. I grab it expecting to see the email but it's a message from Jez.

How are you doing now mate. Meet for a drink later.

He is so needy. But I'm going to keep him waiting for a reply. Jez is a problem and I'm not sure how

I'm going to handle him.

I flick back to email, still no sign, then, just as I'm about to put the phone down again it appears. I click on the link and it takes me to a page to change the password. I'm not on the app though, this is a website. I flick back to the app and am just about to try the relevant letters of the new password when it occurs to me that I should shut it down and reopen it. But something stops me from opening it again and I flick back to the website.

I'm still logged in. I check through the site, looking at Micky's profile and security. That's when I see it; a menu which contains the options to reset the password but also to reset the memorable information. I wonder if that is what the app is wanting me to input, specific characters from the memorable information? I grit my teeth as I click on the link then change the memorable information. I have to scribble the info, along with the new password, on a scrap of paper to make sure I don't forget either.

Gingerly I open the app again, wondering if this is a good idea then I type in the relevant characters from the memorable information, cross my fingers and wait. It seems to take a long time though probably is no more than a few seconds.

It lets me in.

Micky's accounts, because there are several of them, appear in a list alongside the balance for each. I click on the current account – our joint account – and scroll down the transactions. I can see my wages going in regularly, and Micky's too. I can also see that his redundancy payment has already come through. There are debits for utilities and the mortgage, as well as withdrawals for cash amounts, presumably to pay Mik. I can even see the debit card transaction for my recent shopping trip. There's also a regular amount disappearing every month to another account. It's a savings account and there's also a lot of money in there, as well as an ISA. We're not poor at all, we never have been. All those extra shifts I've worked while heavily pregnant were unnecessary.

Why did he make me do it?

Given how frequently Micky went to the pub, and how much he drank, I'm astonished there's so much money. But when I look back at the transactions and see Micky's wages going in, I understand why. He earned so much more than he led me to believe. It explains why he received so much redundancy money.

I keep looking through the transactions. I can't believe my eyes. I had no idea we had so much money. Admittedly most of it has come from Micky's earnings and Micky's savings, but I have made a contribution, and given all the extra hours I worked, it's not insignificant.

My marriage was a sham. It certainly wasn't built on trust. If things had been different, if Micky hadn't been such a drinker and, as it turns out, a liar, would he still be alive today?

Only if he hadn't tried to rape me, a little voice in my head says.

And he murdered our baby.

And I murdered him.

I'm not the only bad person to live in this house.

I'm contemplating my future. I'm contemplating my past. Until Mum died it was fine. Then I was on my own, once the *care* system had spat me out. I've done okay but not as well as I would have done if Mum had still been alive. But I managed; I fed myself, I worked, I always had somewhere to live. Admittedly it was never glamorous, cosy like home had always been with Mum, but it was dry and, most crucially, not on the streets; I never slept rough.

I glance around the shabby living room of the house Micky bought, because, if I'm honest with myself, he chose it. I may have signed the forms and have my name on the mortgage, but everything else was his decision. To be fair to him he did put down the lion's share of the money, my only contribution to the deposit was a thousand pounds which I did lots of extra shifts at the supermarket to accumulate. And, of course, he paid the lion's share of the mortgage because he earned the most.

Now I'm stuck here. I can't possibly sell, can I? Not with Micky's body in the foundations. It's my own fault.

And Micky's.

I'll have to stay and make this house as comfortable and cosy as I can. And I'll have to keep working to pay that mortgage, but I do have a sizeable amount of money to fall back on. Thanks to Micky.

There's a rapping on the front door, loud and

insistent and it makes me jump. I get up and attempt to see out through the living room window but the angles are wrong and I can't see who's knocking. They rap again. I'm not expecting anyone, I haven't ordered anything online. I don't want to answer. Rap again, louder this time.

The police?

There is no putting it off. They won't go. And I might as well let them in and face my destiny. Maybe a neighbour saw us bury Micky's body after all.

Taking a deep breath I march into the hall and open the door.

'Oh.'

'Is he in?' Jez looks annoyed and impatient.

'Um, well…'

'I need to speak to him because he can't be arsed to answer my messages.'

Damn it, that's my own fault. I had intended replying to Jez, I'd just got side tracked and hadn't done it yet. I shouldn't have made him wait so long.

'Oh, mate,' Jez calls, looking past me and into the kitchen.

My already increased heartrate thumps even faster in my chest, in my ears. Slowly I turn around and see Mik in the kitchen, just come in from garden, unsuspecting, unawares. Jez's addled brain has affected his eyesight. Although, with the daylight behind him in the dingy kitchen Mik could be mistaken for Micky. If you squinted.

Mik's hand goes up in a wave.

'I've been messaging you. You've hardly replied. Didn't reply at all today.' Jez's tone is angry and accusing. Needy. 'I was beginning to think you was dead.'

'Dead,' I say, with a laugh. I don't think it sounds hysterical.

'So,' Jez says, ignoring me. 'You coming out for that drink now or what?'

Eleven

There's a faint kind of whooshing noise that travels down the hallway and into the kitchen.

Or maybe it's in my head.

'Can't, mate,' Mik says.

I do a double take, he sounds so like Micky, so like him.

'I've lost me job. I'm giving up the drink. I need to be on me own with Cal. Sorry.' He turns then and steps outside, closing the door behind him.

'Fuck me.' Jez shakes his head. 'Is he ill?'

'Yeah. Liver thing…' I mumble.

'He looks shit. Fuck me.' He turns and ambles up the driveway, past Micky's car and off down the street. I watch him for perhaps a little too long, before I close the door and deadlock it, suddenly worried he might turn back and barge in.

I run out into the garden to find Mik leaning against the wall he's just built. He looks shaken.

'Sorry I came inside, I didn't know…'

'It's alright, he fell for it. He really thought you were Micky.'

Mik nods his head slowly.

'I don't think he'll come back in a hurry.' I really believe it too. 'He did say he thought you looked awful, or rather Micky looked awful.' For some unfathomable reason I'm finding it hard not to snigger. It's totally inappropriate and I don't know what's wrong with me.

Mik purses his lips together. If I didn't know better I'd say he was struggling not to laugh too. 'I was good, wasn't I?' he says.

'You were. I'd have been fooled by the voice. How did you do it? How did you sound so like him?'

'He talked to me a lot. I listened. I suppose I just soaked up the way he spoke.'

'Do it some more. Say something else.'

'Like what?'

I ponder for a moment or two. 'Say, "I'm not going to the pub again, Cal. I've given up the drink.'

He repeats my phrase and I cannot believe what I'm hearing. 'You definitely paid attention to Micky's voice, didn't you? Have you always been able to mimic people?'

He shrugs. 'Sometimes,' he says. 'Depends how they speak. And I can't keep it up for long. It's tiring.'

'Would you like a coffee?' I head back to the kitchen and he follows me.

Inside, leaning against the kitchen cupboards hugging our coffees and eating biscuits, I openly scrutinise Mik. He's about the same height as Micky, slighter in build, and today he's wearing the grey jumper he found stuffed behind the cushion when we were hunting for Micky's keys. Maybe Jez saw that, maybe it helped to convince him he was speaking to Micky.

'Is everything okay?' Mik asks, watching me watching him.

'Yes, fine. I just can't get over how easy that was, fooling Jez. Although he is a drunkard so maybe he's an easy person to fool.'

'I wasn't trying to fool him,' Mik says, sounding defensive. 'I just realised by coming indoors I'd messed things up for you. When he spoke to me I had no choice…'

'I'm not criticizing. I'm grateful. Jez has always been a nuisance, a bad influence. Especially lately.'

Mik finishes his coffee and puts the cup in the sink. 'I'd better get on. The roof trusses come tomorrow.'

'Ah, do I need to pay for them? I'll need to get the cash out. Or could I pay the suppliers with my card. I probably could. That would be better…'

He holds his hand up to interrupt me.

'What?'

'I've already paid for them. They're made to fit so had to be paid upfront.'

'Okay, how much do I owe you? You prefer cash, don't you? I can go now and get it, depends how much it is, there's a daily limit I think, not sure how much it is…' I'm babbling on, remembering that he doesn't have a bank account.

He holds his hand up again.

'Wait until they arrive, then you can see the invoice.' He goes back outside and I go into the living room.

There's a text from Jez on Micky's phone.

Mate sorry to see you so ill. You look like shit. When will you be better? Next week?

Oh, so it seems that Jez isn't going to give up so easily.

It takes me almost twenty minutes to compose Micky's response, racking my brain for the turn of phrase Micky might use, as well as flicking through old texts. When I'm happy with it, I finally press send and cross my fingers.

Sorry mate. I prob won't be able to share a pint with you again. Got some liver damage and docs say alcohol is off the menu. Got to be careful now. Losing my job ain't helped.

I hope it'll be enough to ward him off for now while I think about how to push him away permanently.

But, it seems, Jez isn't going to be deterred.

Mate I could pop round with some beers. You could just have one. What about this evening?

Damn him. I send a reply before he gets any more stupid ideas and turns up on the doorstep again.

Kind offer mate. But no thanks. I cannot have even one beer. You trying to kill me, ha ha. Anyway, promised Cal I'd take her to the cinema tonight. Have one for me mate.

After I press send I wait to see if there is any response, but after half an hour there isn't. Which I hope is a good sign and means he's finally got the message. But, just in case, I need to be out tonight.

Mik leaves after his day's work and I hurriedly tidy myself up ready to go out. I've decided I'll drive over to the supermarket on the other side of town again and look around the clothing section. I could do with some new clothes, clothes that actually fit me. I haven't had anything new in months, just stretching my normal clothes over my growing baby bump. Micky was reluctant for me to waste money on new clothes because, as he pointed out several times, I'd soon spring back to normal and then they would be no good. Ironically, he's right there, I'm thinner than I've ever been, but not because I've had a baby. Quite the opposite really.

I'm ready to leave, having decided I'll get some cash out in readiness to pay Mik even though I don't know how much the roof trusses are when it dawns on me that I need to use Micky's card, since his is the one that usually draws out cash and I don't want any suspicious activity on our account.

But, of course, I don't know the pin number.

I'll use my own card but I'll do my shopping first; if it gets refused at the cashpoint machine I'd rather it was after I've done my shopping. But I do need to think about what I can do about Micky's card; I need to use it otherwise it will look odd.

It'll look as though he's dead. Not that anyone is checking I suspect but you never know. Computer algorithms and all that.

I get into the car and back it down the drive, it feels strange to be driving again, second time in a week. Micky never really wanted me to drive unless it suited his convenience which usually meant when he'd had a skinful. It's fortunate that I'd already learned to drive before I met him because I don't think he would have been supportive of me learning.

Not, I remind myself, that Micky's opinions matter anymore. Once I'd passed my test I rarely drove because I could never afford to buy a car, let alone run one. That's another item for my list, find out what happens with the car, I know it has to be insured and taxed and MOT'd; I need to find those documents.

As I drive around the corner and past the little car park near the end of our street I notice a van that looks just like Mik's, maybe he's just stopped to make a few phone calls. He's that type, conscientious, law abiding; he wouldn't use his mobile while driving.

Well, maybe not completely law abiding.

On my trip, which I really enjoy, I buy myself a few tops, two dresses, a decent pair of jeans that actually fit me and some new trainers as well as picking up some more food supplies. I've spent more on clothes on this one trip that I've spent in the last year in total. As I think of this on my way home I wait for the feeling of guilt to hit me, but it doesn't. For the first time in a long time I almost feel happy.

And a little guilty I suppose. But not for feeling happy, just for killing Micky. But what's done is done and cannot be undone. Am I a psychopath? Is Mik? I don't feel much remorse, that's for sure. And it's not as though Micky was a drunken wifebeater. It only happened once. Then there was the rape. That only happened once too – mainly because we killed him before he really got going. But if he hadn't died would he have continued behaving in that way?

I'll never know.

I do a double-take as I approach the car park at the end of my street, Mik's van is still there. Maybe it's not his van just a similar one. I slow down as I pass and make a mental note of the number plate.

I'm opening my bedroom curtains when Mik's van pulls up the next morning. By standing on tiptoes and squinting I can just make out the number plate. Yes, it matches the van I saw last night. It was him.

I step back and watch him walk up the drive, he's carrying his tools in a large leather bag. He doesn't look up and he doesn't see me but I nip downstairs just in case and open the kitchen door just as he arrives at the extension building.

'Coffee?' I ask, feeling cheery. I'm wearing my new jeans and one of the tops.

'Morning,' he says. 'Coffee, please. And can I use your bathroom?'

'Of course.' I turn away to fill the kettle but out of the corner of my eye I notice that he takes a small bag from his tool bag before heading upstairs.

I can smell the toothpaste on him when he comes back down.

'Are you hungry? I'm just about to make a bacon sandwich; would you like one?'

His face lights up as he tells me he would love one, before going back outside. I'll call him in when it's ready.

I take our plates as well as tomato and brown sauce through to the dining table, then call him in. I've made a large pot of tea too.

‘Wow,’ he says.

I’ve made him two sandwiches, double what I have. ‘I thought you looked hungry.’

‘Yes,’ he replies, through a mouthful of food.

I pour us both a cup of tea and push his towards him. He eats both his sandwiches and drinks his tea faster than I manage half of my sandwich.

‘You *were* hungry,’ I joke.

He nods, stands up, says thank you and takes his plate with him.

‘You look really nice today,’ he says, just before heading back outside.

When I take a cup of tea out to him later he’s balancing on a ladder manoeuvring what I assume is a roof truss into position. It’s quite ingenious how he’s doing it, one end supported by a prop thing. He glances down at me as I approach.

‘That looks like a two-man job,’ I joke.

‘I can do it.’ He carries on manoeuvring the structure until he’s happy with it.

I must admit that just looking up to where he’s balancing makes me feel a little dizzy, yet he seems perfectly at ease up there. It’s obvious that he’s done this many times before.

He comes down and takes his tea.

‘How many more are there?’

He shrugs and smiles and nods over to the corner of the garden where several more are stacked up.

‘I would offer to help but…’

‘It’s fine. I can do it.’

I’m grateful for that. I suppose he doesn’t have

any help because it would cost more and he doesn't have the mechanism for paying people, although I'm sure many would be happy with cash in hand.

'Would you like to stay for dinner this evening?' I ask, making it sound much grander than it really is.

'Yes please,' he says, handing me his empty mug. Then he winks at me and climbs back up the ladder.

I'm not sure what to make of that.

Twelve

After I've rummaged through the freezer, defrosted some chicken, and created a stew which I've put in the oven on a slow heat, I decide I need to tackle the issue of Micky's debit card. I need to be able to use it, if only to draw out cash.

I spend a jolly hour going through the banking app on Micky's phone before giving up and getting my laptop out; I don't use it very often and it's old but still works just fine. There seem to be more links on the website than there are on the app, either that or I can see them better. After much rummaging around – I really need to get up to speed with this online banking – I finally find what I'm looking for.

I order a new pin number for Micky's card – a step in the right direction.

Mik comes in from the garden a little earlier than expected but the jacket potatoes I've put in the oven to go with the stew aren't quite ready.

'Oh, hi, err, not quite ready yet.'

'Could I use your shower?' he asks.

'Of course.' I follow him upstairs and find clean

towels for him. 'Have you got clean clothes with you?' I doubt it since all he has with him again is, what I assume is, his washbag.

He shakes his head. 'These are okay, I'll put them back on.' He grimaces a little.

'Don't do that. Let me find you something of Micky's.' We both flinch as I say this, but then he nods his agreement.

Going through Micky's wardrobe, while my accomplice in his murder is showering in the bathroom, is a surreal experience. Eventually I find what I think is suitable, choosing clothes which were tighter on Micky than he'd have liked them to be, including underwear. I leave them outside the bathroom door and go downstairs to the kitchen.

When Mik appears I turn and catch my breath. In Micky's clothes, just for a second, he *is* Micky, especially as he doesn't seem to be shaving much these days and has the beginnings of a beard. 'It's nearly ready,' I mumble, covering my shock. 'Why don't you go through to the table.'

We're both quiet as we eat our meal. Again I've given him twice as much as I've given myself. He eats as though he's starving.

I tell him to stay seated while I take our plates out to the kitchen and bring back some pudding – it's just a shop bought cake. He gobbles up two slices while I look on and stir my coffee.

'You certainly have an appetite,' I say.

'Yes. Sorry. Hungry work.'

'Have another slice.'

He eyes me carefully before taking the slice I've

just cut for him.

Just as he's about to bite into it I say, 'I saw your van in the car park at the end of the road late last night.'

He hovers for a moment the cake still in mid-air, then he bites into it and watches me as he chews, not that cake requires much chewing. He takes another bite, then another, until the cake is gone. I begin to wonder if he has heard me. He finishes and pushes the plate away, then picks up his coffee.

'I said,' I begin, but he interrupts me.

'I know. I heard.' He takes a swig from his coffee.

I wait for him to say something. Anything.

'Are you sleeping in your van?' I know the answer but I need him to say it.

'Yes.'

'Why's that?'

He puts his coffee cup down and stares at me. 'Landlord kicked me out.'

'Why? He can't do that. There are laws.'

He smiles. 'Not for the likes of me.'

'Oh yes. So why?'

'I owed him rent.'

The penny drops and I feel myself sinking into my seat.

'You didn't have any cash to pay him because I haven't given you any. Why didn't you say? You said it wasn't a problem.'

'I didn't think it was. But he put the rent up and wanted to backdate it. We had a row. He kicked me out. Not a problem. I find somewhere else.'

'But how? Won't another landlord want

references, bank details, that sort of stuff?' I know about renting; I've done enough of it in my time and even the dodgiest landlords that I came across always wanted to check my credentials even if their own were suspect. They always wanted to protect themselves.

'It's fine.'

'It's clearly not or you wouldn't be sleeping in your van.'

'I'll sort something out.'

I nod then get up and go out to the kitchen where I fill the sink and start on the washing up. I'm thinking, I'm contemplating, I'm miles away when suddenly he's there, picking up the tea towel and drying the dishes. He's a lot more helpful that Micky ever was.

'You could stay in my spare room,' I blurt. 'Until you find somewhere else.'

'No. Not possible.'

Now I wished I hadn't suggested it.

'Have you found somewhere else already?' By already do I really mean since I left the table? Anything is possible, I suppose. He could have made a phone call.

'No, but I will, soon.'

I pull the plug out of the sink and dry my hands. 'The offer's there. The room isn't doing anything else.' Though I will have to clear it of the baby things, which I must do whether he stays or not, but I admit I've been putting it off.

'Why are you so kind?' he asks, hanging the tea towel on its hook, a hook put there many years ago by a previous owner.

'I can't have my builder sleeping rough now, can I?' I try to make it sound like a joke.

'Can I think about it?'

'Of course you can. But don't take too long, there's probably a queue of people waiting to use that room.' Another joke, though not funny.

He leaves shortly afterwards, saying a soft goodbye and thanking me for my hospitality. He looks embarrassed, I feel embarrassed. I do wish I hadn't said anything, left him to his own devices, minded my own business.

But it's hard because we're entwined now whether either of us likes it or not.

After he's gone I find his dirty clothes in a neat roll on the bottom of the stairs, he's obviously forgotten them. I don't know how long he's been wearing them because I never took much notice but judging from the smell, several days. I throw them in the washing machine and set a timer on my phone to remind me to take them out when done so they can be tumbled dried and he can wear them tomorrow. I don't want him mixing cement in Micky's decent clothes.

'You didn't show me that invoice,' I say, as I hand over his clean clothes.

'Invoice?'

'For the roof trusses.'

'Ah yes. You have washed my clothes?'

It feels awkward between us again, just like last night. 'Yeah, they were stinking the place out.' I laugh and slowly he joins in. 'You can use the bathroom to change and clean your teeth,' I say, sounding flippant.

I go into the bathroom after he's finished and he's left Micky's clothes in a folded pile on the toilet seat.

Last night's talk of the spare room, even if my offer of help was rejected, has made me twitchy about it. I stand at the door looking at the bed covered in baby things, unopened packets of nappies, little clothes on coat hangers, the unassembled cot against the wall. No matter what, I need to sort this room out, I can't have everything lying around as a constant reminder of what might have been. I have to move on with my life no matter what's happened.

Micky might still be alive if the baby had survived.

If he hadn't raped me.

I'm going back to work at the end of next week so I need to tackle this now.

Two hours of hard work and a few tears and I've cleared the room, made the bed, dusted and hoovered. I stand back and admire my handiwork. The room is now ready.

A little voice asks: ready for what?

Who knows, just in case.

I've put the baby things at the top of the built-in wardrobe. I hadn't realised how high the cupboards were, going right up to the ceiling. I think on the plans these wardrobes remain after the extension, which is good because not only are they useful they look good too, unlike the rest of the house. I've pushed the cot pieces under the bed.

'Did you sleep okay last night?' I ask, when I take him a cup of coffee mid-morning, because he looks tired.

He shrugs.

'Have you got that invoice?' I remind him again. 'I need to sort out what I owe you so far. Then we need to have a chat about how much it's going to cost to finish the building work.'

He nods, rummages around in his pocket and hands it over.

'Are you okay?' It's finally dawned on me that he's hardly said a word since he arrived.

'Just tired,' he says, with another shrug.

I give him a sideways look but now *I* don't say anything. I waiting for him to say more which, after a little while he does.

'There were some kids in the car park late last night.'

'Oh.'

'Just skateboarding. I can see why, smooth surface, no cars, except for my van in the corner. But they were a bit noisy. I had to move in the end.'

'Where did you go?'

'Side street.'

'I've cleaned and tidied my spare room, the offer is still there. I feel it's my fault you're in this position because I haven't paid you. Micky would have paid you, wouldn't he?'

'It's okay,' he says, without really answering my question.

'Well… make sure you're not too tired to work. I don't want you falling off your ladder.'

After I've studied the invoice I realise that it's going to take me quite a few trips to the cashpoint to withdraw enough cash.

I don't see much of Mik for the rest of the day as I take myself off shopping again, I'm starting to really enjoy this. Although I mostly buy food and toiletries. I seem to be running low on those – probably all that time I spent in bed after losing my baby when Micky did as little as possible and certainly didn't think to buy toilet rolls or shower gel. I draw out as much cash as I can again on my debit card and hope that Micky's new pin number arrives soon.

'Would you like to stay for dinner again?' I've brought supplies to cook something a bit more special that a stew.

Mik looks at me for a long moment. God, he looks tired.

'Yes. Please.'

'And feel free to take a shower. And would you like some more clean clothes? Save your work clothes for tomorrow.'

He looks at me, his eyes doleful, his smile small, and nods at me.

'You go on up, I'll sort out some clothes.'

Now he's sitting opposite me exactly where Micky used to sit on the rare occasions we sat at the dining table, and wearing some of Micky's clothes again. If I focus my eyes into the distance and away from him he could almost be Micky. As I whip our empty plates away and back to the kitchen I notice his neatly piled work clothes on the stairs again. Nestled on top are his keys. I swipe them up and put them in the cutlery drawer. I don't want him sleeping rough in his van another night – he looks like death warmed up and I don't want another death on my conscience. Not that Micky's plays on it much.

He eats pudding in silence, enjoying every mouthful but too tired to speak.

'Sit over there and watch a bit of TV while I clear up,' I tell him.

'I can help.'

'No, really, sit down. You've been working hard all day.'

When I come back he's asleep on the sofa, his head pressed into the headrest. I flick the TV on and watch a reality show without really seeing it.

It's late when he suddenly jerks awake, almost midnight.

'I should go,' he says, stumbling up from the sofa.

'Stay.'

'I cannot.'

'Why not?'

'It would be wrong.'

'In what way?'

'You are a married woman.'

'But I'm not, am I?'

Thirteen

He's been sleeping in my spare room for almost a week now.

He didn't put up much of a fight that night, muttered something about not being able to find his keys, then needing to use the bathroom before he left. I showed him the room, he almost fell on the bed and the rest, as they say, is history.

It's been surprisingly easy. He's easy to live with. Undemanding, tidy, cleans up after himself, happy to help with washing up and washes his own clothes of which there were many festering in his van. But I don't mind.

I've paid him now too. We're fully up to date on the stage payments. He's also insisting on paying me for his accommodation, which seems very bizarre, but I've given up arguing. I'll just save the money and give it to him as a cash bonus when the building work is complete. It's coming on in leaps and bounds now the roof is on and the building is weatherproof.

I'm up very early today, showered and dressed in

my supermarket uniform because today is my first day back at work. I really don't want to go but I have to. Everything has to appear normal. While no one I work with would notice Micky's absence because they've never met him they might notice any out of the ordinary behaviour from me. Not going back to work after I've worked so many extra shifts to pay for this wretched extension would look odd. Also, I do need to pay the mortgage. Despite all the money Micky's accumulated, I do need an income.

Mik is already working away. He's doing as much as he can before he has to knock through because, he says, that is going to be chaos. I can't say I'm looking forward to it but at least if I'm at work I'll miss the worst of it. I hope.

I'm taking the car because, why not? No one is going to notice or ask. I've checked the insurance document which took a lot of finding because Micky kept everything like that secret – I don't know why. I found it in a tin box on the top of his wardrobe. It also contained various other documents as well as his driving licence and passport. He looks so young on his passport photograph, but he would have only been about thirty when it was taken. His passport is due to expire the month after next. I won't be renewing that. But I don't think the passport office will think it's odd, he hasn't been abroad since I've been with him. Anyway, do they even check things like that? I very much doubt it. *I* don't have a passport, never needed one.

Work is what work is. Everyone is being very careful with me because they all know why I've been off. No one mentions babies or children or anything that might upset me. And I'm working the dayshift with no extras at the moment, eight to four with half an hour for lunch. The time goes by quite quickly and I find myself feeling slightly guilty for not feeling guilty about murdering Micky. This feeling only hits me occasionally.

Odd, isn't it? I have no remorse. Definitely something wrong with me because I really loved Micky to start with. Or, as least, I think I did. Anyway, what's done is done and can't be undone – that seems to be my mantra. And me going to prison and Mik getting deported and going to prison or whatever would happen to him is not going to bring Micky back. I expect all murderers excuse their crime like that, but it's not as if we're serial killers. It's not as if we're going to do it again. Micky was a victim of circumstances. Circumstances of his own making.

We all were.

As I let myself in through the front door I smell something nice. Food. It makes my stomach rumble.

'What's going on?'

Mik is standing in the kitchen stirring a pan on the hob.

'You've made enough meals for me. My turn now.' He gives me a shy smile. It's really quite endearing.

He's really quite endearing.

'It'll be ready soon.'

'Do I have time to change out of my uniform?'

He nods and smiles. 'Quickly,' he says.

The food is on the table when I return. It's some sort of meat curry, not too hot but very spicy. Micky wasn't a lover of spicy food so we rarely had it. I rather like it although my mouth is fizzing when I've finished.

He whips our plates away and brings back a pot of tea.

'No pudding?' I grin at him.

I've never made puddings.

'There's ice cream, I think I need some to cool my mouth.' I go to stand up but he puts his hand up.

'No, you sit. I'll go.'

Afterwards, when we've washed and dried up the dishes together and are sitting on the sofa watching nonsense TV, he pulls Micky's phone from his pocket.

I frown.

'You left this behind,' he says.

'Yes, I never intended to take it to work.'

'It rang and rang. I could hear it. In the end I had to come in and look.' He pulls up the missed calls list and hands it over to me.

Before I look I can feel panic rising in my chest. What if it's the bank? What if they've realised Micky isn't about anymore?

But the list of missed calls is Jez. One after another, minutes apart for about ten minutes. That was late morning and there's been nothing since.

'Damn him. At least he gave up eventually.'

'He left voicemails.'

'Oh.' I flick through the text messages to access

the voicemail. Mik puts his hand over the screen.

'You don't want to listen to them.'

'Why not?'

'You don't.' He shakes his head. 'I messaged him.'

'Did you?' I say, flicking through to text messages.

Mate. Cal's already told you I'm ill. I can't drink alcohol ever again. It'll kill me. Being with you is too tempting. Please don't call again. Sorry mate but that's the way it is. Also, don't talk about my wife like that. Ever.

I'm stunned by the message.

'I looked back over old messages between them to see what he usually writes.'

'He hasn't replied so let's hope he's taking it seriously.' I pause then before continuing. 'What did he say about me?'

Mik shakes his head.

'Just give me a summary.'

'No. You don't want to know.'

'I can listen to the messages.'

He grabs the phone from me and clutches it tightly.

'He says nasty things. He's not a good man. Please don't listen to them.'

I suppose Jez blames me for Micky not wanting to see him. If only he knew the truth, but thank God he doesn't. Right then the phone rings and Jez's name flashes up on the screen.

'He hasn't given up,' I say, taking the phone back from Mik, accepting the call and putting it on loudspeaker before placing it on the coffee table in front of us.

'Micky, that you, mate?' Jez's raspy voice asks. He

sounds as though he's already had a few.

'No, it's me.'

'Callie,' he says. 'How are you? Good now?'

'Yes, thank you.'

'Is he there? How comes you're answering his phone? Got him on a tight leash, eh?'

'No.'

'Can I speak to him then?'

'He's busy.'

'Yeah? When will he not be busy. I want to see him. He's my mate too. I've known him longer than you. Have you got him locked up? Have I got to come round there and release him from his prison?' He laughs now, a horrible, guttural cackle.

I feel alarmed. Supposing he does just turn up? I jump up, looking outside because it wouldn't surprise me if he was out in the street now. But fortunately there's no sign of him.

'Put him on, Callie. I want to speak to my mate.'

'Hey mate, you all right?' Mik says, sounding just like Micky.

'Micky, me old mate, me old mucker, how are you?'

'Been better.'

'What's actually wrong with you then?'

'Got this liver thing. Got to keep off the drink. Be dead in three months otherwise.'

'Mate, that's shit.'

'Yeah,' Mik says.

'You can still come out though. Drink coke while I down the pints for us both.' Jez cackles again and then we hear him slurp his drink. He's probably already drunk, actually probably never really sober which is good because Mik's near perfect impression of Micky is starting to waver.

'Seeing you is too tempting, mate,' Mik says. 'I can't do a pub again. Ever.'

'I'll come round. Bring a few beers.'

Our eyes meet over the phone, alarm in both Mik's and mine.

'No, mate, no. I have to leave that all behind.'

'And you're leaving me behind. Some mate you are.'

'Sorry, mate.'

'Is she making you do it? I know what a bitch she can be. You should have left her like you said you were going to. You've saddled yourself with a right cow there.'

'Don't talk about my wife like that,' Mik says, and ends the call.

My heart is beating rapidly in my chest, I feel a little faint, a little sick. What if Jez just turns up?

'Is he married or anything?' Mik asks.

'No, I don't think so. I don't think anyone would tolerate him.' I don't add that Jez is a bigger drinker than Micky was, and he was bad enough. But, I chide myself, it's not as though I didn't really know. I met him in a pub when he was propping up the bar and downing beer as easily as water.

'Why do you ask?'

'We don't want him badmouthing you to his partner or questioning Micky not being around. Where does he live?'

'I've never been there but I think it's a flat over

an off licence, something like that.' I've never asked Micky about Jez, mainly because I've never been interested. I suppose if he were to say anything to anyone it would most likely be John, the pub landlord, or anyone in the pub who would listen. I try to remember what that pub was like, how busy it was. It all seems so long ago. Were there many other hardened drinkers around? Was there a group of them? Either way has advantages and disadvantages. If there was a group then Jez will not be a lonely drinker, equally he's probably shouting the odds about Micky's absence. I don't want people wondering and questioning. Although the liver disease thing is a good excuse. I pull out my own phone and Google liver disease.

'What's that?' Mik asks, frowning.

When I tell him he frowns harder.

'Since we've invented this illness that Micky has, we need to know something about it. It says weight loss and confusion are some of the symptoms. That could be useful.'

'You're not going to pretend I'm your husband, are you?' He laughs lightly.

'I think that ship has already sailed. Jez was certainly convinced. Not that he's a good measure being constantly under the influence. But you do a good impression of Micky. If I close my eyes even I could be fooled. Have you always been good at that?'

'Maybe. A bit. I used to do my uncle. He would laugh.'

'When did your uncle die?' It sounds so brutal when I ask that I wish I hadn't. 'What I mean is you must miss him.'

'I do every day. But he isn't dead.'

'I thought you said he was. I'm so sorry.'

'I might have said he's gone, because he has gone. The dementia so bad he doesn't know his own name never mind mine.'

Fourteen

He looked so sad after he told me his uncle had dementia that I never pressed him for more information. I just leant over and squeezed his hand and he squeezed mine back. We're a pair of sad souls who have been brought together by a tragic event. Well, that's how I'm choosing to frame it anyway.

I've been back at the supermarket a week now; I don't hate it. I don't love it either. The only light at the end of the tunnel, or day I should say, is that when I get home he's there. Mik. He's cooked every day I've worked. He says he's not the best cook and doesn't know many meals, but they're tasty and warming and filling and Micky never did anything like that. Ever.

The aroma of something tasty makes my stomach growl as I open the front door. I can hear him in the kitchen, he's singing to himself; a song in a language I will never understand. His voice is surprisingly high, unlike his speaking voice. He stops when he realises I'm standing in the kitchen doorway. I can't hide the smile on my face.

‘Sorry,’ he says, grinning at me.

‘No, it was lovely.’ I’m not sure lovely is quite the right word.

He narrows his eyes at me before turning his attention back to his pots on the cooker. ‘I found a book today. I hope you don’t mind.’

‘A book?’

‘Recipes,’ he says, nodding to the book wedged open on the worktop. He’s used a couple of tins to hold it in place.

I have a sudden flashback to the sardine tin that I didn’t hit Micky with though I would have done if I’d had the chance. I let out an involuntary gasp.

‘Sorry, is it special?’

‘No, no. Not at all.’

‘But you looked sad. Is it special book?’

‘No. It was my mum’s but no, it’s not special. What are you cooking?’

He glances over at the book. ‘Pork chops with green beans and mashed potatoes,’ he reads out.

I laugh. It seems quite a basic meal to need a cookery book for. I can’t remember my mum ever referring to it but I found it among her few books after she died. There was a Jane Austen and how to look after your baby book too.

‘Sounds delicious. Have I time to change?’

‘Be quick.’

When I come back down he’s putting our plates on the table. We eat every night at the dining table in the living room. It’s become our habit very quickly. It’s easy, it’s comfortable. He is easy and comfortable.

'Did your mum make this often?' he asks.

I laugh. 'Not that I recall. We were more into pizza and pasta.'

'Oh.' He looks crestfallen.

'But this looks fantastic. I mean, what a treat. When did you get the pork chops?'

'Yesterday. At the butcher shop, not the supermarket.'

While we're eating I tell him about my mum, the young single parent who raised me all by herself and wanted better for me that she had for herself. I tell him how kind and warm she was. What a great mum she was and all the plans we made for my future, my education.

'Where is she now?' he asks.

'She died,' I tell him. I'm grateful that I've finished my food by this point because then I start to cry, big ugly tears sliding down my face.

He comes around to my side of the table, crouches down and hugs me tight. It feels nice. It feels good.

I give him my life story, how I've survived on my own, meeting Micky, our wedding, Jez.

So now he knows everything about me.

He makes us a coffee and, unusually for us, we sit on the sofa while the washing up soaks in the sink rather than washed and dried immediately.

I'm holding my coffee mug up to my mouth and feeling foolish and vulnerable. There's a strange atmosphere between us. Embarrassment probably.

His and mine.

'I do miss him,' he says, his voice barely above a

whisper.

'Your uncle?'

'Yes. He was my saviour. Without him I would be dead. He paid the traffickers.'

'Oh my God, I didn't realise.'

'He paid enough for my whole family but only I got out.' He goes quiet now, staring into the distance. His breathing has become rapid and shallow. Then he cries silently.

I reach over and grip his hand. He looks at me and forces a painful smile. Then he goes off to the kitchen, I hear him blow his nose. He returns and offers me another little smile. 'Sorry about that.'

'Don't be. Tell me your story.'

'I was seventeen, tall as I am now but thin.'

'You're hardly fat now.' It sounds flippant and I wish I hadn't said it.

'My uncle took me in. Looked after me. Became a father to me. I was the child he never had. He was married once, but she died young, he never remarried. He employed me in his building firm, which makes it sound big, but it wasn't. At one point I was going to claim asylum. We looked into it. Then he told me not to.' He stops.

'Why?' I prompt.

'There were rumours, friends, relatives of friends. They'd tried to claim asylum and been sent back or had to disappear. My uncle said I was safer hiding in plain sight. So that's what I did. I have no, what's it called, print, imprint.'

'Digital imprint.'

'Yes, that too. I don't exist. It was never a

problem when my uncle was well. He took care of everything. Then, as time went on I started to take care of everything, but always in his name. Then he flipped one day when I was at work. Came home to the police. He'd been found driving the wrong way down the motorway. Lucky no one was killed. After that I became even more invisible.'

'But you own a van, you drive; you must have a driving licence.'

'No, I don't. Never had a lesson other than from my uncle, never took a test.'

'But you own a van, and a smart one too.'

'In my uncle's name. Insured in his name too. I have all the documents except a driving licence. I keep the van serviced. I pray I'm never stopped by the police or in an accident. I'm careful.'

'But how do you pay for that if you have no bank account?'

'My uncle's account.'

'You still have it?'

He shakes his head. 'No, not since he went into the home. Then the social services and the council and official people took over. I was just a lodger in my uncle's home as far as they were concerned. They gave me notice to quit. Served it to me. Legally.' He laughs slightly, bitterly.

'You gave them your real name?'

'Of course. What difference it make? I don't exist. Untraceable.' He follows this with a little shrug. 'Before they got their hands on everything of his, I took what I needed. Things of value, sentimental. Documents. Photos. There wasn't much really and I had nowhere to put it. They took the big things, the furniture went to charity, all his belongings other than what went to the nursing home with him.'

'So where do you keep all these things?'

'In my van. Now some in your house, in my bedroom.'

'Safer here than in there.'

'Yes, much safer. But the van was safer than the room in the house. Nothing was safe there. I'm glad I'm here. I feel safe here.'

There's a silence while we both evaluate what he's just said. Finally I break it. 'I'm glad you're here too.'

'What will you do when your van insurance runs out? How will you renew without a bank account, without a credit card?'

'I'll think of something,' he says, with a little grin. 'Not everything is online or on the phone.'

'No.' I think of the brokers in our high street, the last remaining one. 'I suppose you can turn up with a wad of cash,' I muse.

'Yes.' He smiles at me again. 'I think I'll wash up now.'

He washes and I dry. I sense he's talked enough about his past but I can't let it drop.

'How long have you been here? I mean your English is so good. Your accent only comes out occasionally. And you're a good mimic.'

'Twelve years,' he says, handing me a plate to dry. 'I spent all my time with my uncle and his friends, no English friends, but I watched TV.'

I quickly do the maths. 'So you're twenty-nine.' A little younger than me although I thought he was a lot older. He has that weary, wary look in his eyes. He's probably seen a lot, been through a lot.

'Thirty,' he says. 'I had a birthday last week.'

'You didn't say. We should have celebrated. We still could.' What the hell am I saying?

'I prefer to keep a low profile.'

'Yes, of course. But we could go out for the day. Go to the seaside. Walk along the beach, feel the wind in our hair.' Some of the girls at work had been talking about beaches, about looking forward to the summer, wondering if it will ever come. Maybe that's what put the idea in my head.

'It's March,' he says, laughing lightly.

'Yes, but it's nice, it's spring. It's not supposed to rain tomorrow and it's my day off. You could take a break from building and we could go. Just get up and go. Eat fish and chips. Say yes,' I say, sounding as though I'm pleading. The truth is I could do with a break too. Do something different.

Get away from Micky's dead body.

It takes us less than an hour to reach the beach; I drive. The sun is shining intermittently, forcing its way from behind little clouds. It's windy and we wrap up warmly, I even wear gloves. Mik is wearing one of Micky's coats, I forced him to bring it when I realised that his own was dirty from building work. It fits him well now because he's gained weight since he's lived with me.

We walk along and feel the air in our lungs. It makes me feel alive. I hold out my arms and spin around. He laughs, as he pulls down his hat to cover his ears.

'Cold wind,' he says, by way of explanation.

I nod and agree. I laugh. So does he.

I feel free. I feel unburdened.

I don't feel guilty about Micky. I know I should.

We spend an hour in the wind and sun and sand and sea spray, then wander into the town and around the touristy shops. I buy a shell, a large one that most certainly has not come off this beach but most likely a one far away in a hot country.

'Did you come here often?' he asks.

I know what he's asking. 'With Micky, you mean?'

'Yes.' He looks intently at me.

'No. He wasn't one for days out unless it involved a pub crawl. Not my idea of fun. If only I'd realised how incompatible we were he might…' I let the words trail away. I don't need to say them.

'Yes. Maybe.'

'Fish and chips?' I say, changing the subject.

We decide it's too windy to eat them on the beach and find a little sea-facing fish restaurant instead.

'I've never been to the beach here before,' he says, as he studies the menu.

'Always been my favourite. Used to come with Mum. On a coach.' I smile at the memory. 'It made for a long day as a kid, but I loved it.'

'I've never been to a beach in this country at all.'

'Really? But you've been here for years. Did your uncle never take you? What about days out with friends?'

'My uncle didn't like days out, or holidays. And I never really had those type of friends. My uncle's friends were my friends.'

'Oh. I see. We'll have to come in the summer when the weather's nice.'

He stares at me for a moment too long. I feel my face flush as I realise what I've said.

'One more stomp along the sand before we head home,' I suggest.

He nods his agreement. He looks happy. The happiest I've seen him since I've known him. He's taken his hat off because the wind has dropped a little and constantly pushes his hair out of his eyes.

'You need a haircut,' I say, laughing.

He runs his hand through his hair. 'Yes, I do.'

We decide to head home and instead of walking to the far end of the beach to use the ramp or steps, Mik leaps up onto the promenade. He's tall and he's done it in one go. I look up at him and shake my head.

'You can do it,' he says.

'No.'

He holds out his hand and I take it before I scramble up the wall which mostly consists of him pulling me. It's an ungainly process but when I finally achieve it, we both start laughing.

'Callie, Callie,' a female voice interrupts us. I ignore it. No one would be calling my name. 'Callie.' The voice is closer now. 'I thought it was you.'

I blink into Sam's face. Sam from work; she's older than me and nice though I don't think of us as friends, just colleagues. 'Hi,' I mumble, feeling like a kid who's been caught skiving off school.

'This is Paul, my husband,' she says, indicating a man holding a little boy's hand. 'And this little rascal is our grandson, Oscar.' She grabs his other hand as if owning him. Before I get a chance to say anything she says, 'And this must be your husband, Micky, isn't it?'

Mik steps forward and says hello. Somehow, we are still holding hands.

'You obviously had the same idea as me, all that talk about beaches yesterday made me want to be on one. Bit cold though. We're off soon. What about you?'

'Yes,' I agree. 'We're just heading back to the car. Better go before our parking ticket runs out. See you at work.' I smile my brightest smile and pull Mik away.

'Bye,' Sam calls behind us.

Neither of us mentions the mistaking Mik for Micky, not in the car and not when we get home.

Fifteen

'Are you okay?' I ask Mik as we're busy cooking a meal together.

Although cooking is perhaps not quite the right description. We've moved the microwave into the living room and are nuking up ready meals because Mik has started the knock-through which means the kitchen is like a bomb site. He says it'll get worse before it gets better. He'll be knocking through the dining room, which admittedly we don't use, next.

'Fine, fine,' he says, smiling.

'Okay.' But he clearly isn't okay. I can feel his twitchiness; he's almost nervous. It takes several hours until he finally confesses.

'I did something bad today.'

'Bad?' I feel a little alarmed but remind myself that it cannot be as bad as what *we* have done.

'I was coming back from the builders' merchants when I got stopped by the police.' He looks away from me, not wanting to meet my gaze.

'Why? What did you do? I thought you were always careful.'

'I am. I am. It was one of those pull-in things. They were stopping lots of drivers.'

'Okay. What happened?'

'They ask questions. When did I last have a drink. That sort of thing. They check the van.' I can tell he's stressed because his accent is stronger and he's missing out words.

'You were fine then?'

'Yes. Even if I did drink alcohol it was middle of the day. No one drink in middle of the day.'

I almost laugh. Micky was not immune to the pull of the pub at lunchtime, although he never got drunk, he was too seasoned a drinker for that. Mik, the innocent, wouldn't understand though.

'They asked for my name. Asked if I had my licence with me.'

'Oh shit.'

'Yes. I said I didn't think so.'

'What about the insurance?'

'They already knew the van was insured.' He's still looking away from me.

'Did you give them your name?'

'No. I just made a show of hunting through the car, the door pockets, the glove compartment. Then I panicked and used this.' He pulls something out of his pocket and turns to face me.

'Shit,' I say, when I see him holding up Micky's driving licence. Sometimes I give him Micky's debit card to get cash. I trust him and anyway, it's easy to know how much he's drawn out because I can check on the banking app. I'd just handed over Micky's wallet this morning because I was in a hurry. 'What happened?' I can feel my heart thumping in my chest, even though I know I haven't done anything wrong, not in this case anyway.

'She looked at the picture, looked at me, and took it off back to her car. Then she came back a few minutes later, handed it back…' He stops speaking now but I can tell he wants to say something else.

'Well… Did she say anything else?'

'She said it expires soon and I should make sure I renew it. Once she'd said that she said I could go. And she waved me off.'

'She was checking it against the police computer. Making sure you, well Micky, wasn't disqualified, I suppose. Which he wasn't to my knowledge.' Though God knows how because he must have driven while over the limit on more occasions than I could count, even if he wasn't rolling drunk. 'Let me see.' I hold out my hand for the licence.

It's an old picture, Micky is younger and leaner than he was when we did what we did. I glance between the licence photo and Mik's face. I don't think they're that alike, but then I knew Micky's face better than most. I suppose there is a passing resemblance especially if you factor in the passing of time and that this is an old photo. In fact, Mik looks more like this photo than Micky did before he died.

He pulls Micky's wallet out of his pocket and hands it back to me. I stuff the licence back inside.

'The insurance must have been okay,' I muse. 'I'll check later.'

'My van is insured.' Mik sounds almost indignant.

'Yes, but Micky isn't named on your insurance, is

he? He must have 'drive any car insurance' on his own, ours.'

Later, when I check, I find that is the case, thank God, or we'd be in some kind of trouble now.

I've spent all night tossing and turning. My mind has been on overdrive. I'm worried that Mik is going to get caught properly another time. Then he would be deported I assume. Is it too late for him to apply for asylum? I have no idea about these things.

The extension will be finished eventually, maybe in as little as a month, then he will move on and will not be my problem. Except that we will always be each other's problem. We're bonded together by what we did.

Also, I don't want him to leave.

I like having him here. I like it far more than I ever did when living with Micky.

'Shall we do something tomorrow, like we did last week. It's my day off,' I say, over breakfast.

'But it's not my birthday.' He stops and ponders for a moment. 'Is it yours?'

'No. No. It doesn't have to be a special occasion just to go out, does it?'

'Okay.'

We've had another lovely day out, a walk around a lovely picturesque village, lunch in a charming *olde worlde* pub and now we're home and exhausted.

'That was the best day,' Mik says, handing me a cup of tea.

'It was.' It really was. Far better than any day I

ever spent with Micky.

Mik drops down on the sofa next to me and rests his head on my shoulder. 'Thank you,' he says.

'What for?'

'For showing me nice things.' He sits back up and grabs his own tea, he uses a giant builder's mug.

'That's such a cliché,' I say, meaning the mug.

'What is cliché? What have I said?'

'No, I mean the mug. You're a builder and you drink builder's tea out of a giant mug.'

He frowns at me, then grins. 'I am a builder.'

'You are. And thank you for today too. I really enjoyed it.'

He takes one of my hands and grips it. 'I've had the best of times with you lately.'

'Me too.' I don't add that we've also shared the worst of times because we both know it.

Our eyes meet and he smiles, it's a little, shy smile. I know where this is leading and I have to decide if I want it to or not. But my body makes the decision for me and I lean towards him. As our lips meet I know this is right, wrong, and yet so right.

We slid into bed last night, my bed, both of us. It was the best of nights. I was apprehensive; it was the first time since I lost the baby – if you don't include Micky's barely begun rape. But I needn't have worried, everything was fine. Better than fine. With Micky it was always a bit frenzied, a bit urgent, especially on his part. With Mik it is easy, comfortable. He takes time. He isn't hurried. The first time was good, the second better and after that

I lost count.

'I need to get up for work,' I moan, pulling the covers up over us and snuggling into him.

'Me too,' he says, kissing the top of my head. 'But I'd much rather stay here with you. Spend the day in the bed.' He laughs and goes to get up but I pull him back.

'Then let's.'

'You have work.'

'I can throw a sickie and you can please yourself.'

'Tempting,' he says.

'We're doing it.'

It's been two weeks now since that day. Mik sleeps in my bed every night, it has become our bed. We're enjoying spending more and more time together. He told me he loved me. I said it back. It is the truth.

'I've made a decision,' I tell him one morning over coffee in the kitchen. 'And if you agree it could solve a lot of your problems.'

'What problems?' He frowns.

'Well, the biggest problem of being illegal,' I say.

'It's okay. I manage. I survive.'

'Yes, and that's something else we need to work on.'

'What is?' He's frowning so heavily now that his brow is deeply furrowed.

'Your accent, your speech.'

'But you said it was good.'

'It is. Most of the time. But sometimes when you're tired or stressed it slips. And you miss out the odd word.'

‘I don’t, do I?’

‘You do. But never mind, we can work on that. My idea is, and I hope you like it…’ Suddenly I feel foolish, embarrassed even for what I’m about to suggest.

‘Yes?’ He waits for me to continue.

‘I think you should become Micky Fisher. Properly.’

He shakes his head. ‘I don’t understand.’

‘Well, his passport is up for renewal soon. Then his driving licence. And you could be him.’

‘How can I?’ He shakes his head again.

‘Wait there.’ I run off and find Micky’s soon to expire passport. I flick through to find the photo page and thrust it at Mik. ‘See. It’s ten years old, that photo. I think you could pass for him now. We’ll style you up a bit and take some photos and well, give it a try.’

‘And what happens if it doesn’t succeed? What then?’

I have to admit that I hadn’t thought about what might happen if this doesn’t work. It’s not even crossed my mind. Which, on reflection, seems ridiculous. ‘It will,’ I say, confidently. Because I really do think it will. ‘And once the passport goes through, we’ll do the driving licence. Then you can sell your van to Micky and reinsure it legally and well, there you go.’ I keep my voice breezy. ‘And I’m going to apply for a passport at the same time. I’ve never been out of the country, unless you count Wales, and who knows we might want to go on a little holiday.’

'O-k-a-y,' he says slowly. 'But what does it mean? I mean, how will things change?'

'You'll be legal. No one will be able to deport you. It won't even occur to anyone to do that because you'll be British born Micky Fisher.'

He nods slowly, taking in everything I've said. 'And I'll be married to you.' He stares at me intently, his brown eyes focused on my face.

'Oh, yes. I hadn't thought of that.' I have though, I very much have.

'Will I still be me?' he muses, more to himself than me.

'You'll always be Mik, not Micky. Don't worry, you don't ever need to pretend with me. In fact, I never want you to be Micky.'

'What about his family?'

'I told you before, they haven't been in his life for a very long time. I don't think they even know where he lives.'

With that we both glance outside. Only *we* know exactly where Micky lives now.

Sixteen

I bought no-alcohol champagne just for this occasion. It was on offer at work, plus staff discount, so very reasonable.

'Cheers,' I say, chinking my glass with Mik's. 'It's amazing.'

He grins at me. 'You like the colour?'

'I love it. I'm glad I trusted you and let you choose.'

We're standing in the master suite. This is the first time I've seen it finished. The bed arrived today along with all the furniture which we've chosen together, but Mik chose the colour for the walls. He wanted to put his stamp on our home.

The extension is finished, all the building work completed and signed off by the council building inspectors. All legal and above board.

Just like Mik.

His passport came back today too, so it's a double celebration. He's been grinning since he opened the envelope. He is now officially Micky Fisher, British citizen. Next is his driving licence.

'You'll have to choose the bedding and curtains,' he says, putting an arm around my shoulder and hugging me to him. 'You are definitely better at that than me.' He kisses the top of my head.

'We can go together on my next day off.'

We have plans to decorate the entire house; we've already done the kitchen/dining/living space. It's enormous, much bigger than I ever imagined. Micky – that is the original Micky – had quite the eye for design. Even the tumble dryer has a proper home tucked away alongside the washing machine in their own little laundry room. I'm grateful to him for giving us such a lovely home. It's like something out of a magazine.

'Once I've finished painting all the rooms I'll start on the garden. It's a right mess because of all the building work, but it will be bloody lovely.'

I laugh. Since Mik agreed to become Micky we've been working on his speech. Micky wasn't a prolific swearer but he did drop the odd bloody into his sentences so now Mik is peppering his speech with them. We've been watching old videos of Micky on my phone to get the pattern and accent right. Sometimes when Mik's speaking and I'm not looking at him I could swear that it's Micky talking.

'Drink up, we've a whole bottle of this stuff to drink and it won't be the same tomorrow.'

'No? Why?'

'It'll be flat.' I chink my glass with his again and grin at him, but he doesn't grin back.

'That bloody Jez rang today,' he says, putting a complete dampener on our mood. We haven't heard anything from Jez in months. I thought we were free of him.

'What? I thought he'd got the message. Damn it. Damn him. Did you speak to him?'

'Yes. I told him not to call again.'

'Do you think he'll do it; not call I mean?'

'He was drunk, slurring his words. So I don't know.'

'Nothing we can do.' I sigh. I thought he'd got the message. 'He's such a pisshead,' I say. 'As long as he doesn't come round here.'

'What if he does? What will I do?' There's alarm in Mik's voice.

'I'll deal with him. I'll send him away with a flea in his ear. I might as well live up the reputation he's given me.'

'What if you're not here?'

'Don't answer the door.'

'He could go to the police. He could report me.' Mik sounds more and more concerned.

'Ha, and what could he report you for? You have a passport. You are Micky Fisher.' I hug him tightly. 'Don't worry. That pisshead will never be believed.'

'What if they involve other people?'

'Like who?'

'People Micky worked with. Or down the pub.'

He has a point. I hadn't thought of that but I have to reassure Mik. 'You're overthinking it. Just don't answer the door. It's months since he last rang, isn't it? It'll be months more or maybe he won't bother us again.'

Three months later

Unbelievable news, I'm pregnant. We weren't trying but equally we weren't avoiding it either. I took the test twenty minutes ago. I've been feeling funny and I suspected I knew what that feeling was and I was right. Mik cannot stop grinning. Every time he looks at me his face breaks out into an even bigger grin. I feel the same way. I'm only just pregnant so we're not telling anyone.

Ha, who am I kidding, we've got no one to tell. Other than work but that is a long way down the line. I'll be asking for light duties when the time comes and definitely won't be working extra shifts.

'What do you think it'll be?' Mik asks as he sits me down at the giant kitchen island – thank you original Micky Fisher – and pours me a large orange juice.

'It'll be a baby,' I say, giggling.

'Very bloody funny.' But he laughs.

I can't believe how happy I am about this. Really cannot. When I became pregnant the last time there was a lot of stress. I put off taking the test for weeks because I didn't know how Micky would react. He was okay with it but not before he called me a stupid mare as though he had nothing to do with it. But now, with Mik, this is different. He's ecstatic.

I've suspected for days but I wanted to wait until my day off before I did the test. The last thing I wanted to do was go to work feeling thrilled but not able to talk about it, or worse, go into work feeling sad.

'Coffee?' Mik asks. 'You are allowed coffee now?'

'Yes please and yes in moderation.' I'll have to get out the pregnancy book I bought the last time. I've flicked through the one my mum had for me but it's so outdated.

'I'm so bloody happy,' Mik says, coming over for a hug. 'Thank you so much. You made me the happiest man alive.'

'*You've* made me the happiest man alive,' I correct him, then giggle back. It's rare now that he drops words, only when he's stressed or, as today, excited.

'Yes. Of course. So bloody happy.'

He sits next to me and we stare out into the garden, holding hands and grinning. I'm so bloody happy too.

Everything in our garden is rosy. I mean that both literally and metaphorically. The garden is a testament to Mik's hard work and, previously unbeknown to him, green fingers. Micky could never have achieved so much and in such a short time too. I know nothing about gardening but I do know how to appreciate the colours, the variety and abundance. I admire it every day and Mik loves it.

He's fully legal now, has a driving licence, *sold* the van to Micky Fisher, has it fully insured correctly too. Everything is above board.

Well almost.

We haven't forgotten what we did. How can we? But we don't talk about it much and when we do we have a sort of shorthand for it. A look, a nod. To be honest I find it hard to believe that Micky is buried beneath our beautiful kitchen and I don't think I could accurately say where exactly he is. Mik probably could because he did the digging. When I look back on that night it's a blur and the blurring is increasing as time goes on.

Mik is still working hard on other people's building works. He's had to increase his prices because now he's legal he has to pay tax. But it's okay. He still gets the jobs. Between us we've set up a Facebook page and he posts pictures of work he's completed; he runs adverts too. His page is called Mik's Bricks. I came up with that. He's even managed to get a line of credit at the builders' merchants although not at the one he used to use but a different one so they don't question his name and circumstance change. It's lucky we live in such a large town and there are several builders' merchants.

Life is good and I've never been so happy, far happier than I ever was with Micky even in the beginning when times were good.

Do I feel guilty about what happened? I ask myself this occasionally and wait for a sinking feeling but it never comes. I've even stopped justifying it to myself. We did what we did, it cannot be undone. It's unfortunate.

Am I a psychopath? Is Mik?

Maybe.

We're just finishing our breakfast and Mik is loading the dishwasher when the phone rings. It's Micky's phone. We keep it in the kitchen and charged up. It's probably ridiculous but I keep it because I don't want anything to look odd. I use it for online banking although I do have the banking app on my own phone now too. Mik doesn't use it at all; he has his own phone for his business. Micky's phone rarely, if ever rings. Micky's colleagues were just that, colleagues and they haven't kept in touch. His only proper friend was Jez.

When it rings we both stop and look at each other. Then Mik picks it up.

'It's him,' he says, and I know instantly who he means.

'Don't answer.'

Mik rejects the call. Immediately it rings again. I shake my head and Mik rejects the call again. We both wait for a third ring. There's a longer gap and we're starting to think he's given up but then it rings again. Mik glances at me.

'Let it go to voicemail,' I tell him. It's ironic that the voicemail is Micky's voice and he was obviously feeling rough the day he recorded it because it's a growled-out message that just says, 'Leave a message.' I can't imagine why anyone would bother after hearing that.

But Jez will.

'What timing he has,' I mutter. 'Bastard.'

'Should we listen to it?' Mik says, his voice soft.

'I suppose we should.'

'Hey, mate. It's me. Your old mucker Jez.' He doesn't sound drunk but it's not even nine in the morning, even Jez can't start drinking before breakfast, surely. 'Just saying I haven't heard from you. Saw your missus driving your car the other day, not the first time either. You still alive? I have me doubts. Might pop round with a few bevvies. See ya.'

'Oh God.' I feel sick at the thought of it.

'I'll text him,' Mik says, picking up the phone.

'I don't think that will do it. I think you'll have to ring, to prove you're not dead.'

Mik sighs. 'Now?' he asks.

'Yes, get it over and done with, we don't want him coming round here, do we?' We discuss what he's going to say and rehearse it a few times.

He calls Jez, puts the phone on speakerphone again and sits it on the table in front of us.

It goes straight to voicemail and judging by Mik's face he's as relieved as I am.

'Hey, mate,' Mik starts as we both wince. 'Just to say I got your message. No, mate, don't come round here. I told you I'm not drinking. Me and Cal are making a go of it. Going bloody well. Sorry but there it is and I really don't want to discuss it with you.' He ends the call and we grimace at each other.

'We should go out.' I stand up. 'Go out and enjoy ourselves.'

'In case he comes round?'

'That and to celebrate our news. Don't let that pisshead spoil it for us. Leave the phone here so we can't answer even if he does ring.'

We pack up quickly, collect what we need and load ourselves into the car.

After a lovely day at the seaside where we've walked and talked and eaten and laughed and done our best not to think about Jez, much less talk about him, we head home.

We drive down towards our house, we're singing *Oh I Do Like to Be Beside the Seaside*, an old song my mum used to sing to me when I was a kid, and one she said her mum sang to her. I've been trying to teach it to Mik all the way home. I hadn't realised quite how tone deaf he is, unlike Micky who, even when drunk, could carry a tune well.

I stop singing mid-song. 'Keep driving, keep driving,' I yell, as we approach our drive. Fortunately Mik sees him at the same time as I do and sails carefully and sedately past our house.

Jez is slumped on our doorstep. He looks as though he's nodded off to sleep.

'Did he see us?' Mik asks as we head down to the bottom of our cul-de-sac.

'I don't think so. But I'm worried about turning around and driving past the house again.'

'We park here.' He pulls the car into one of the parking bays. I've never parked the car down here before because there's never been any need but Mik often parks his van here and fortunately has today. He tilts the rear-view mirror then plays with his wing mirror. 'I can see the drive now. We'll wait until he goes.'

'I hope it's soon; I want to go to the loo.'

An hour passes and Jez is still sitting there. I'm sure he's asleep.

'I don't think I can wait much longer,' I tell Mik. 'I really need the loo.'

'He's still there. He hasn't moved. Do you think he's dead?'

'Ha. We should be so lucky. Just drunk.'

'We could drive round to the pub, you can use the toilet and we could have a drink, I'm so thirsty.'

I laugh lightly. Until he met me Mik had never been in a pub. His uncle didn't frequent them because he thought they were sinful places, as a consequence Mik felt the same. So he was pleasantly surprised, proclaiming that it wasn't a sinful place at all. Now he loves a pub lunch, even though neither of us drink alcohol.

Mik starts the car, then immediately switches it off again. 'Duck. He's standing up.' We both crouch down and hope he doesn't look our way.

'Maybe he's going,' I whisper.

'I don't think he can hear us.' There's amusement in Mik's tone.

'He's checking his phone. He's looking around, keep down. He's stamping his feet. Ah, he's moving, he's gone out of the mirror view now.'

Has he gone?' All I can think about it going to the loo.

'Can't tell. Can't see him. No. He's sitting back down.'

I open the car door.

'What are you doing?'

'I'm going to get rid of him. You stay here and keep your head down. I'll ring you when the coast is clear.'

Mik grins as I say this. I grin back. It's almost fun.

'Jez,' I say, as I approach my house. 'What are you doing here?'

'Waiting for Micky.' He casts suspicious eyes over me.

'Oh, well you'll have a long wait. He's away.' I look down at the carrier bag Jez has, it's full of beer cans. I can see that he's drunk most of them.

'Away where?'

'Work.' I slide past him towards the front door, key in hand.

'He lost his job.' Jez's tone is challenging.

'Now he has another one.'

'I'll come in and wait,' he says, standing up.

Luckily, I still haven't opened the front door. 'No, you won't. He's away overnight.'

'He's not answering his phone.'

Damn it, the phone is still sitting on the kitchen worktop. 'He is. But not to you apparently. I spoke to him ten minutes ago.' Take that, Jez.

Jez takes a few moments to take in what I've just said. 'Right.' He starts to stand up, though it's more of a stagger. 'Can you tell him to ring me? Please,' he adds, as though it hurts.

'I'll ask him. Anyway, I've got to go now. You'd best go home and sleep it off.'

'You couldn't resist could you, Callie? Always the little snipe. Micky always says you have to have the last word.'

I shrug. I don't know whether Jez is telling the truth or not, but it doesn't matter because Micky doesn't say anything at all now. 'Bye then.' I open the door, slip inside and close it after me.

I desperately want to run to the loo but I can't because I have to wait and watch and make sure that Jez does leave.

From the living room window I watch as he weaves his way down the street, occasionally stopping and glancing back. He checks his phone again before carrying on. I will him away, mentally pushing him further from our home and our life. Finally, he rounds the corner and is out of the street. I run to the loo, when I get back I check for any signs of him. Then I ring Mik and tell him to leave the car in the parking bay but to come home.

'I'll have to ring him later,' Mik says after I fill him in. 'Do you think he'll ever give up?'

I shake my head slowly. 'No, don't ring him.'

I think we should move to another town,' Mik says, hours later when we're lying side by side in bed in our lovely bedroom.

I think he might be right.

Seventeen

Almost eight months later

'Push, Callie, push. She's almost here now.' The midwife's professional face looks down on me and smiles.

'You said that an hour ago.'

'Not an hour ago, Callie, about ten minutes.'

'Feels like an hour,' I mumble as another contraction grips my body. I feel as though I'm being torn in half. We didn't realise I was in proper labour and left it too late to come to the hospital, so it was too late for the epidural which I definitely wanted.

'Head's born,' the midwife says.

'Oh my bloody God,' Mik says, daring a look from over my shoulder but not venturing down the *business end.* He was horrified when I told him that he'd be at the birth. 'She's got black hair.'

I can't reply because I'm too busy pushing the rest of her out. Then, suddenly, she's here and she cries.

'Is she all right? Is she?'

‘She looks just perfect,’ the midwife says, plopping my baby’s hot little body onto me. ‘Do you have a name for her yet?’

‘Yasmeen,’ Mik says, a little too quickly. We’ve discussed this at length, he wants to call her after his mother, which I understand but I’ve told him that Yasmeen doesn’t sound like a name Micky Fisher would choose. We’ve agreed on Jasmine as a compromise, although I prefer Esme, after my mum. So that’s *my* compromise.

‘Jasmine Esme,’ I say.

‘Jasmine Esme Fisher,’ the midwife repeats, as she writes my baby’s name down. ‘We’ll get her weighed once you’ve delivered the placenta.’

I keep looking at her, her little snub nose, her chubby cheeks, her dark brown eyes. I thought all babies were born with blue eyes, but that’s not true at all.

‘She smiled at me,’ Mik says, tickling her chin.

‘I think that might be wind.’

We’re getting ready to leave the hospital. I’ve had an overnight stay and although I’m desperate to get home, I’m also apprehensive. I keep telling myself everything will be fine.

‘Did you bring the chocolates up?’ I ask Mik.

‘No, I left them in the car. I’ll go and get them. Will you be all right?’

‘Of course.’

During the time he’s gone I manage to finish dressing myself and pack up all our belongings. I’m settling Jasmine into the baby car seat Mik’s brought up when a midwife comes over to check on us.

'Oh yes, she's snug in there. So much better when a baby is a good weight.' She smiles at me and pats my arm. 'Mum okay?' I'm about to say that no, she's dead when I realise she means me.

'Yes, thank you.' If I sound nervous, she doesn't pick up on it.

Then she starts giving me information about babies, appointments, health visitors and clinics. It's all very general and I'm only half taking it in when I see Mik's ashen face appear behind her, he looks shaken. I want to tell her to stop talking but I can't really do that.

Finally she moves away and Mik catches her and offers the chocolates and a thank you. She turns and smiles her thanks at us both.

'Are you okay?'

He shakes his head.

'I saw him.'

'Who?'

'Him. Jez.'

'What? Where?'

'In the entrance hall by that big information desk. He was in a wheelchair.'

'Oh. Did he see you?'

'I don't think so. I held the chocolates up to my face. I must have looked odd.'

'But he didn't see you?'

'I don't think so. Do you think he would think I'm me, Micky, I mean?'

'I don't know. We don't want to chance it.'

We've had several more phone calls, a lot of texts

and two visits since the day he camped on our doorstep. That's why we have to move. We have to go where he cannot find us. We've been lucky and clever enough to get rid of him without making him anymore suspicious, but there will come a time when our luck runs out. Typical of him that on one of the happiest days of our lives he pops up again like a rotten stink.

'It doesn't matter. We'll soon be far away.'

'Yeah,' Mik says. 'We will.'

We should have moved house three weeks ago, but typically the date has changed. Some problem with the buyer's mortgage which unsettled us as we thought, irrationally but also naturally for us, that somehow Micky's body under the extension had been discovered. But it turned out to just be a technical issue with lending dates. So now we're moving next week. For definite. I don't know if that's better or worse. It's hard to say, moving while heavily pregnant or with a newborn? Either way, it's happening.

We sold the house to the highest bidder. Three people were interested and I couldn't believe the price we got. All that building work was definitely worth it. I'll be sorry to leave the house, because it is almost perfect. Except for the obvious. And Jez.

I must admit I was very nervous when the estate agents came round to value it, and even more so when the buyer's surveyor came. But Mik pointed out that no one would ever know, well, not unless they demolished the extension and who in their right mind would do that?

We're moving to a town thirty miles away. The house we're buying is smaller than ours but Mik has already started talking about an extension to the kitchen. But there's no immediate hurry because the house is neat and tidy and not the bombsite tip that was the house that Micky chose. So there's plenty of time to change it when we're ready.

I was surprised how easily we got a mortgage too. Although it's mostly based on my supermarket earnings – I've transferred to the same chain in our new town. I'm not sure I'll even go back to work, but the mortgage company believed me when I said I would. It certainly helped that we have a lot of savings and a lot of equity thanks to the profit we made on our sale. Mik has been earning more than enough to cover any mortgage payments, but of course he'll be starting from scratch again when we move to a new town. I'm not worried about money at the moment. I'm going to enjoy my baby for a while.

Unlike the last time. Because I'll never forget my little boy. Or what happened to him.

Mik lifts the car seat onto the buggy wheels, picks up my bags and waits for me as I take the brake off and start to push our baby towards home. It feels weird. And wonderful.

We're soon out of the lift and heading towards the entrance and there's no sign of Jez. I'm looking left, right and centre scanning the area for him and so is Mik.

We both breathe a sigh of relief. He's gone. We're safe. We amble down towards the car park and Mik bundles my bags into one hand and puts his other arm around my shoulders. I glance up and I see the look of adoration on his face as he stares down at our daughter.

I'm so happy. We're so happy.

Then I spot him and I stop so quickly that Mik almost falls forward.

'What?'

'It's him. Over there.' I point with my head.

Jez is still in the wheelchair, one leg extended in front of him and encased in a blue cast. A woman wearing a *volunteer* tabard is waiting with him, probably ready to whisk the wheelchair back. They're waiting by the pick up and drop off area.

I wheel the buggy in a wide arc away from Jez and head back towards the hospital.

'We'll go in the café,' I tell Mik. 'And wait until he's gone.'

I get a window seat in the café so I can keep an eye on Jez while Mik goes and gets us both a drink. If we were ever to drink alcohol, it would be now. But of course we don't.

Jasmine is sound asleep and I hope she stays that way. She was fed over an hour ago and should be fine, but she's new born and hungry and could wake up. Without conscience thought I start wheeling her back and forth, just to give the illusion of movement.

'Still there?' Mik puts our drinks on the table.

I nod.

He sits down and faces the window too.

'I wonder how he did that? His leg, I mean,' Mik says.

'Drunk probably.'

He nods. I take a sip of a drink I don't really want and keep rolling the buggy back and forth.

We sit for a long time just watching cars arrive, getting excited because we think Jez is being picked up, then feeling deflated when he isn't. Finally, after almost half an hour a white people carrier stops and between the driver and the volunteer, Jez is heaved into the back of the car. He doesn't look as though he's helping himself at all. He's facing us while this all happens. A pair of crutches are heaved in after him, the car pulls away and the volunteer wheels the chair back.

'Do you think he saw us?'

'No,' I say, reassuring myself as well as Mik. 'We only saw him because we were looking for him. He didn't see us.'

'No.'

'Anyway, even if he did he doesn't look capable of popping round any time soon, does he? And we'll be long gone by the time he is.'

Eighteen

Two years later

It's been a sad day today for Mik. He's been to his uncle's funeral.

He said he stayed for too long and chatted to his uncle's old friends. He said it made him nervous.

He didn't even get to arrange the funeral; it was all taken care of via the local council or social services or some nameless person who didn't know his uncle, maybe even the care home. He doesn't know, just as he doesn't know if all the proceeds from his uncle's house have been spent. He has no rights with regards to his uncle's estate. There was no wake afterwards either so those who attended, who only knew about it because a notice was placed in the local paper – probably protocol – lingered longer around the flowers at the crematorium. I asked him if cremation was okay for his uncle, he said it was because his uncle was a Christian. I don't know what Mik is; I've never asked. It has never come up in conversation. But then, he's never asked me.

I don't think psychopath is a religion. If it is it's mine too.

'They were all still there when I left,' he tells me when he comes home. It's taken him almost an hour to get back because of the traffic; there are roadworks on the main route from our old home to our new one in Whittleham and it's caused a lot of tailbacks.

Mik has travelled that route religiously every week ever since we moved. He never missed a week even though his uncle rarely knew who Mik was. Mik says his uncle didn't know who he was himself either. It's all so sad, him travelling every week and pretending to be just a friend if anyone asked. He says that those rare occasions when his uncle was almost coherent and seemed to recognise him made every visit worthwhile. He's a good, loyal nephew. His uncle had lasted much longer than anyone could ever have imagined but he'd badly deteriorated lately and it was only a matter of time. At least Mik got to see him before he died, literally the night before. When we got the call in the morning from the nursing home, he said he wasn't surprised, sad, but not surprised.

We moved with a newborn, as expected. It was hectic as we had acquired so much furniture by then and added to the baby stuff we filled the removals van. But our new house soon felt like home and we knew we'd made the right decision. The kitchen isn't as big or glamorous as the one we left but it's fine for now. And once Mik had moved the chest freezer out into the garage it was even better. I told him to get rid of it but he says that he'd like to grow vegetables in the garden like the previous owner did. They had an allotment too, we're not going to do that, I've told him and we jokingly bickered about it. We're just like an old married couple.

We've put the past behind us and we're focussing only on the here, the now and the future.

Mik's business is doing well. I never went back to the supermarket, fortunately I didn't need to. I'm a full-time mum to Jasmine and in about six weeks' time she'll have a little brother. We have friends here too, good friends and kind neighbours. We're just your average couple with a young family. Micky and Callie Fisher, although everyone calls us Mick and Cal. We've encouraged them to. No one would ever suspect us of what we've done. To most people we seem very ordinary, almost dull. We're quiet in company, especially Mik. We keep our guard up because you can never be too careful. It's fortunate that we don't drink because alcohol could easily loosen lips, but we don't stress over it too much. We have a good life, the best life.

If I have any regrets it's only that my mum isn't alive to see how happy I am, and to meet her grandchildren. Mik says the same. I think having our own family has really bought home to us how precious our departed ones are. Even though his uncle has not really been with us for the last three years, his death has closed the door firmly on the past.

We're happy.

Mik has decorated the house to our taste and the garden, his hobby, is lovely. We've just had plans passed for a double story extension but we're not in any hurry. We're going to enjoy the baby when he arrives. We have three bedrooms so there's no rush.

Because the baby is a boy I think more and more of the boy I lost. But I force myself not to dwell, we must focus on the present, on the good things in life.

We're going into town together today; we're putting Jasmine in the buggy and we're walking. Mik has a couple of free days between jobs, and the weather is pleasant and it's not too far to walk. Mik is concerned about whether I should walk so far but I've told him, I do it often. I love walking, pushing Jasmine in her buggy is always a treat. That's why we're going into town. We have to order a new buggy. I've been looking at a double buggy, one side a pram suitable for the new baby, the other side suitable for Jasmine. I've been deliberating whether that's the right thing to do but I think Jasmine is still too little to walk everywhere.

'She'll probably have a nap on the way home,' I tell Mik, as we manoeuvre the buggy out of the door.

Mik stoops to pick up the post off the doormat, just the one letter. 'Junk mail,' he says, dropping the letter onto the hall table.

It should only take us about twenty minutes to get into town. The house we live in now is just on the outskirts of the town centre yet there's a lovely park across the road, complete with a lake. Jasmine loves to feed the ducks.

After fifteen minutes in the pram shop we've whittled the choice down to two. We let Jasmine sit in them both, trying them out for size. She giggles when Mik tips the seat back to see how comfortable it will be for her to nap in.

We make our choice, Mik pays and we agree a delivery date in a month's time.

'We should have brought the car,' Mik says, as we leave. 'Then we could have brought it home with us.'

'It's free delivery. We don't want it yet anyway. Let's have a little wander around the shops before we go home.'

Mik groans in jest but nods his agreement.

Whittleham is the kind of small town you see all over England. It's a nice mix of old and new, quaint little alleyways with tiny boutique shops alongside a nice big Iceland and a large Tesco Express. Yes, there are a few charity shops in prime locations but nowhere near as many as where we used to live. And we still have the giant superstore out on its own retail park. I do feel we chose well when we chose Whittleham.

We wander into *Boots* so I can buy a few more essentials for the baby, although Mik thinks we have more than enough. I just laugh when he half-heartedly protests. Jasmine spots some toddler snacks and there's no peace until we buy her something. I sometimes wonder if we are spoiling our little girl then I think I don't care if we are.

I'm at the till paying for the few bits I've bought while Mik waits outside with Jasmine who has started complaining quite loudly because she can't have the snacks until I've paid for them.

I hand over my goods and rummage around in my bag for my purse. I'm just about to pay when something, someone, catches my eye. I look over and see a person who looks startlingly like Jez. I feel my heart start to beat rapidly.

'That's eight-pounds-forty-seven,' the cashier drones, and probably not for the first time judging by her bored tone.

'Yes. Sorry.' I pull my card out and tap it to pay.

She stuffs my purchases into the bag I've just paid for too and hands it over while I scan the area where I thought I saw the Jez lookalike. He's nowhere to be seen.

I'm imagining it.

What the hell would Jez be doing in Whittleham? It isn't him, just someone who looks like him.

'Are you okay?' Mik says when I join him outside. 'You look very pale.'

'Crispies?' Jasmine holds out her little hands and grins at me. I open the bag and hand them over.

'I'm fine. Let's go home.'

'We could get a taxi if you're feeling tired,' he offers.

'No, really. I'm fine.'

'Are you sure?'

'Yes. Just gave myself a fright in there, that's all.'

Mik waits for me to continue. I love that about him, he's quiet and calm, there's never any rushing with him, or urging.

'I thought I saw someone who looked like Jez. Just gave me a scare. Overactive imagination.' I smile at him, take the buggy and march on with conviction.

I feel a lot calmer after a few minutes of walking. Jasmine is happy eating her snack and Mik smiles sweetly at me whenever I glance his way. We turn the corner out of town and I look back, silly really, but I can't shake that feeling. There's no one there. Why would there be? Jez has no idea where we live. We didn't leave a forwarding address with our buyers, just had our post forwarded directly via the *Post Office*. As far as we're aware even our estate agent didn't know our forwarding address. And Jez is unlikely to know who our estate agent was, we never put a board up. I don't think it would occur to Jez to trail through the houses for sale online looking for our old house. Why would he even think we would be moving. We're safe, we're sound, we're happy; I'm just being silly.

But it doesn't stop me looking back a few times.

But it's fine; I don't see anyone.

And we've ditched Micky's old phone. Killed the number, ended the contract. The only person who ever used that number was Jez and he will have got a number unobtainable message, unless it's been reallocated. Not our problem. We've changed bank too and we both have the app on our phones.

Jasmine is asleep by the time we get home. Mik carefully extracts her from the buggy and carries her up to her bedroom. With luck she'll have an hour or two and I can put my feet up.

I wander into the kitchen and put the kettle on. I could really do with a nice cup of tea and a couple of biscuits. I've ballooned during this pregnancy and I know afterwards I'll have to watch what I eat if I want to get back to my normal size again, but I've been so hungry. Mik, who has also put weight on but is still slim, says he adores my bigger body. I don't know if he's being genuine or just kind, but I'll take the flattery no matter what.

Micky would never have said anything so nice.

There's a knock on the door just as Mik comes back downstairs after settling Jasmine and he darts towards it, eager to answer before a second knock might wake her up.

I stop stirring my tea and Mik's coffee and wait to hear who it is. Probably one of our neighbours wanting to borrow one of Mik's power tools, though he has to be careful about what he lets them have both from a safety point and a damage perspective.

When I don't hear anything I wander into the hall.

'Sorry, mate. Thought you were someone else.' It's Jez's distinctive gravelly voice that halts me in my steps. But not before he sees me. 'Oh, Callie,' he shouts past Mik. 'I was right, that was you.'

Oh damn it. If only I'd stayed in the kitchen, he'd most likely be on his way now. It's obvious that when I spotted him in town, he also spotted me. He's followed us home, the little shit.

I stand frozen to the spot. Can I just walk away? Can I pretend I didn't hear him, pretend I'm not Callie?

'Come on, Callie, don't be shy.' Jez, uninvited, steps through the door and elbows Mik aside.

'Watch it,' Mik says, but Jez ignores him.

‘Well, well, well, isn’t this cosy. Look at you.’ Jez is now standing right in front of me in my own hallway. ‘So what’s going on? Where’s Micky? And who’s he?’

Nineteen

Jez has accepted our offer of a cup of tea with three sugars and a slice of the Victoria Sponge which I made yesterday. He looks like he could do with a good meal. We've managed to distract him by making the tea and inviting him to sit in our living room with us.

My mind is racing as I think of what to say. In the end I decide to say nothing. Let him do the talking.

'So where's Micky?' he finally asks, again.

'Gone.' It's not a lie, is it?

'Gone where?'

'I don't know. He just went one day.' Of course I know exactly where he is physically but who knows where his spirit went, to another world? I've no idea.

'When?'

I shrug and look away. He can take that as me being upset if he likes.

'Only he don't answer my calls or my texts. Why d'you think that is?'

'I don't know. I haven't seen him for a long time.'

'He used to answer my calls. He didn't always say

what I wanted to hear but at least he replied. Or texted me.'

'Really, Jez, I can't say why Micky does what he does, like I said, I haven't seen him for a long time.'

'I've been round your old house too, but they didn't know where you'd gone.'

Neither I nor Mik respond. What is there to say?

'What's your name?' Jez spins round to Mik.

Without missing a beat Mik says, 'Mik.'

'That's convenient. Same name.'

'Not quite,' Mik says. 'What are you doing here? Are you stalking Callie?' Nice touch. I do love this man.

'Stalking. No. Not at all. Saw her in town by chance. Couldn't believe my eyes. Thought you was Micky.' He turns back to me. 'You like a type, don't you, Cal?'

'But you followed her home. I think that's stalking.' Mik looks defiant.

'I was following my old mate. I thought you was him.'

'Then why didn't you approach us in town instead of following us home?' Mik isn't angry, it takes a lot to make him angry. In fact I don't think I've ever seen him really angry, shouting angry. Not like Micky.

'I couldn't keep up with you. You walk too fast. When's your baby due,' he asks me, trying to divert attention away from himself.

'Soon,' I say. 'What brings you to this town?' I hope he's just on a day trip.

'Well, there's a story. That's why I'm so keen to

catch up with Micky again. I've given up the drink. Been over six months now. So it would be good to find me old mate. Is he still on the wagon?'

I shrug. 'How would I know?'

'How old is that little tot you were pushing?'

'None of your business,' Mik says, standing up.

'Is it Micky's?'

'No,' Mik and I say in unison.

'So what are you doing here again?' I press him.

'Been for an interview for a job, haven't I. If I get it I'll be moving here, making a fresh start and all that. My doctor says it'll be easier for me not to go back to the drink if I break with old habits, old friends.'

'I didn't know you had any, friends that is, other than Micky,' I snap.

'Yeah, so I'd like to catch up with him.'

'Well, as you can see, he isn't here.' Mik stands in front of Jez in a passive aggressive way.

'So when did he go again,' Jez says, taking a last gulp of tea before standing up.

'Ages,' I say, getting up too.

'Well he was with you that day when I called round and you said he was working away.'

Mik and I exchange a quick glance, and Jez doesn't miss it.

'Caught you out.' He cackles. Drink or no drink his horrible raspy voice hasn't changed, nor his cackle.

'No. He'd gone then. I just hadn't realised it at that point. That's all.'

'What about his stuff? He must have taken his

stuff with him. He must have wanted his money out of that house.'

He has a point and now this is getting complicated.

'It's none of your business but that's why we moved,' Mik says, putting a guiding arm around Jez without actually touching him and ushering him towards the hallway. It's lucky that Mik is tall and Jez is small and weasel-like. 'We still have a few bits of his in the garage, when you catch up with him you can tell him to collect them.'

Mik steps in front of Jez and opens the front door. Jez takes a step forward then stops. He's looking at our hall table, the place where we drop our keys, our post. I'm behind him and I see his hand dart out.

He turns and smiles at me. He's waving a piece of unopened junk mail at me.

'Mr and Mrs M Fisher,' he says. 'What's going on?'

'It's junk,' Mik says. 'It follows you around.' He takes the letter from Jez.

'No, it doesn't. Micky's junk mail would still be going to his old house.'

'We had it forwarded,' I say, which is true though the forwarding service has long expired.

Jez stares at me for a moment or two. 'Yeah, I guess.' He steps through the door and Mik closes it firmly behind him.

Neither of us speaks but he puts him arm around my shoulder and guides me back to the living room. We stand in front of the window to watch Jez wander up the road. He hasn't got very far, barely off our drive; he's obviously a slow walker but we stand there until he's out of sight. We sit down on the sofa together.

I'm in shock. I think Mik is too.

'I'm glad Jasmine was having a nap,' I finally mutter.

'Do you think he'll be back?'

'Don't know. Hope not. But what can he do? Micky isn't here. That's nothing to do with us.'

'No.' Mik picks up Jez's plate and mug and takes them out to the kitchen while I just sit and stare.

Jasmine keeps us entertained for the rest of the day and distracts us from thinking too much about Jez. But he's there in the back of our minds. Every time I look at Mik I can see it in his eyes, just as I know he can see it in mine.

I'm just putting Jasmine to bed when I hear Mik's voice. Who the hell is he talking to? Maybe one of the neighbours has called round but I didn't hear the door go. It's him, I just know it is. It's shitty Jez back to harass us.

Sensing my anxiety Jasmine takes ages to settle, she's normally such a good girl at bed time. Finally, I leave her, closing her bedroom door softly behind me. I creep along the landing and wait to hear voices, Mik's, Jez's. But it's quiet.

I skip down the stairs feeling apprehensive but relieved that I can no longer hear voices.

Mik's face is pale when I find him standing in the living room.

'I thought I heard speaking?'

'Yes, I was on the phone.'

What a relief. 'A work call?'

'Sort of.' He drops down onto the sofa, pats the seat next to him for me to sit too. 'I answer, like I always do saying Mik's Bricks. And this woman's voice asks to speak to Micky Fisher and like a fool I say, yes, speaking.' He stares hard at me now.

'It was him. Jez. He came on the line then, said he knew who I was and I wasn't Micky Fisher.'

'Oh shit.' I rest my head on Mik's shoulder. 'Just when we thought we'd escaped him. He's like a stink that follows us around.'

'I know. Bloody bastard.'

Hearing Mik swear like that almost makes me laugh. I'm the swearer, not him, other than the theatrical bloodies, which he doesn't bother with quite so much nowadays.

'He's on his way round,' Mik says, as he kisses the top of my head.

'When?'

'Now. Literally in the next ten minutes he said.'

'How did he know about Mik's Bricks? We never said anything.'

'Saw the van on the drive, saw the name, the number, the Facebook page. My uncle would never put the name of his building company or phone number on his van, now I know why.' Mik heaves air into his lungs before letting it go in a long sigh.

'No, that's not right. You've got lots of business from that.' Now I sigh, then I deep breathe to calm myself because the last thing I want is to get stressed out and go into early labour. 'Who was the woman?'

'I don't know. It was noisy in there, sounded as though he was in a café.'

'Or a pub,' I say, hoping that Jez has succumbed and fallen off the wagon. 'What are we going to say?'

'Nothing. Let him do the talking because I can't think of a good reason why I have taken your dead husband's name, at least not one that Jez would accept.'

An hour later and we're still sitting on the sofa waiting for Jez.

'Maybe he's chickened out.' As I say it I have my fingers crossed.

'No. Making us sweat, that's all.'

Right on cue there's a knock on the door and Mik jumps up to answer it.

'I'm not making him tea,' I say, standing up too. 'And don't you.'

Jez strides into our living room grinning, Mik follows behind him.

'Well,' he says. 'Isn't this nice?'

I don't reply and neither does Mik. We just stare at Jez, waiting, wondering. I realise that we really have no right to be annoyed or angry with him. Despite being an odious little bastard, he hasn't done anything wrong. We have.

We stand here for what seems like many minutes, the three of us, just looking at each other. I'm tempted to ask him what he wants, but I won't.

'Aren't you going to invite me to sit down?' Jez smirks.

I shrug. Jez plonks himself in the armchair nearest the TV where he sat earlier. I make a mental note to get the carpet shampooer on it tomorrow. Mik catches my eye and nods and together we sit down, me on the sofa, Mik on the other armchair. By unspoken agreement we know that we don't want to look as though we're ganging up on him. Even though we are. We don't say anything even when Jez raises his eyebrows in question. Eventually it's him who speaks.

'So where's Micky?'

'Gone,' I reiterate.

'Gone where?'

'Don't know, don't care.'

Jez turns to Mik. 'Why are you pretending to be Micky?'

'I'm not pretending. I am.'

'You aint. I know Micky Fisher better than anyone and you are not him.'

'It's a common name,' I say.

'Oh come on, Callie, it's not that common. What are the chances of you being with two men with the same name? Bullshit is what you're feeding me. Bullshit. And it's obvious you didn't want me to know neither. You ain't him.'

'No. I'm me. Micky Fisher.'

'Prove it, bullshitter.'

Mik stands up, leaves the room, comes back thirty seconds later during which time Jez and I attempt to stare each other out. Mik thrusts his driving licence in front of Jez's face. Jez makes a grab for it but Mik swipes it away quickly.

'Don't want me to see it's a fake.'

'Nothing fake about that. Nor this.' Mik waves his passport in front of Jez. He's so thrilled with that passport. His British passport.

'Huh, another fake. The police will soon be able to tell.'

'They will and you will look the fool.'

I wonder what he's here for. It's obvious to him that *his* Micky isn't here. And if he's so sure that Mik is impersonating Micky and there's a sinister reason behind it, why didn't he just go to the police? He can't know what we did.

Or maybe he has gone to the police and he's just waiting here for them to arrive. He's going to look a fool when they check Mik's passport.

I hope.

'What do you want, Jez?' I ask, with a sigh. I really could do with an early night, I'm just so tired now I'm in the late stages of my pregnancy. Usually once Jasmine has gone to bed I have a doze on the sofa, cuddled up to Mik while he watches TV or reads the headlines on his phone.

'I want my mate, of course.'

'Well he's isn't here.' I sigh again and look at the clock. It's nearly eight and the light is starting to fade outside. 'Why are you so desperate to find him? Haven't you got anyone else in your life? What about that woman who rang Mik?'

'Oh, her, she was just a woman in the café, smiled at her and she did me a favour. And no, just for your info, I don't have anyone else. He was my buddy, my drinking mate and now we're both sober I want us to get together again.'

I want to say how pathetic that sounds but I don't; no need to antagonise Jez any further. 'Can't you make new friends?' It slips out and I wish it hadn't.

'I'm not like you, Cal,' he spits. 'It's not off with the old and on with the new for me.' He's sitting on the edge of his seat now, rocking back and forth and clearly agitated. I bet he'd love a drink now.

'Would you like a cup of tea?' Mik asks. 'Or something stronger?'

I don't even know if we've got anything stronger.

'Told you I'm off the booze. I'm serious. Don't try to tempt me.'

'I'll make tea.'

I throw Mik a look of annoyance that Jez doesn't miss. I watch the sides of Jez's mouth curl up in a sneer-come-smirk.

I'd follow Mik out to the kitchen and ask him what he's playing at if I could trust Jez, but I can't. Who knows what the bastard would get up to if left alone?

After a long silence Jez finally breaks. 'This new man, this new Micky Fisher, he's not really like my Micky at all, is he?'

I can't even answer that, so I don't, just stare at him and hope he feels my utter contempt.

'I mean,' Jez continues. 'I thought he was, but he ain't. Bit similar looking I suppose. Same type.'

Mik comes in then, thank God. He's carrying a tray laden with mugs – our good ones – our biggest teapot, milk jug, sugar bowl and a plate of biscuits. I can't remember the last time we used that teapot. I hope he washed it out. He puts the tray on the coffee table and starts to pour.

'Milk and three sugars for you, wasn't it, Jez?' That's certainly what he had last time.

'Yes. Thanks. Don't suppose you have any of that cake left?'

'No,' I lie.

Mik holds out the biscuit plate to Jez before he hands me my tea and picks up his own. We sup in silence. It's almost comical. Jez finishes his first mug of tea and Mik immediately offers him another one and more biscuits, because Jez doesn't seem able to take just one, he takes three at a time. For a scrawny man he eats a lot.

'I'll have one,' I say, reaching for the plate. 'Before they're all gone.'

'Not for you, Cal,' Mik says, moving the plate away from me and pushing it towards Jez. 'You do need to watch your weight now.'

Jez sniggers. I snatch my hand away. I feel so hurt; Mik has never, ever said anything like that before.

He sounded just like Micky Fisher. The real Micky Fisher.

Twenty

Jez has had two-and-a-half cups of tea and almost all the biscuits, there's just one solitary one left on the plate. He'd have had more tea if the pot hadn't run dry. He'll be wanting to use our toilet next. I shudder at the thought.

'Someone just walked over your grave, Cal?' Jez says, then right on cue. 'Where's your bog?'

I force a smile though God knows why but it's Mik who points him to the toilet off the hallway.

I make a lunge for the biscuit but Mik grabs it from my hand. He doesn't say anything but his eyes do, soft brown eyes that shine with kindness. I sit back and study the biscuit now back on the plate.

Jez returns and flops back down in his seat. 'That stuff has gone right through me,' he says, cackling.

'You drank enough.'

'Now where was I? Yes, me old mate Micky.'

Here we go again. During the tea drinking and biscuit munching he's asked several times if I have any idea where Micky is: No. How old Jasmine is: Mind your own business. Is she *his* Micky's: No.

'What do you want, Jez?' I ask again. 'If you want to call the police then do it now because some of us need to get to bed early.'

'I don't reckon there's any point,' he says. 'I reckon that you've done some deal with Micky and he's let him,' he jerks his head at Mik, 'have his identity. All I want is to know where Micky is so I can catch up with my old mucker. He owes me some money.'

Finally we get to it. 'How much?' I say as I roll my eyes, I don't even attempt not to.

'Don't be like that, Callie. I know you have money because you was always working all them extra shifts. That's why Micky had to come out with me so often, he was lonely.'

I'd laugh if I had the energy. But I'm not explaining myself to Jez, not telling him that I worked all those extra shifts at Micky's insistence. 'How much?' I ask, now that we've cut to the chase.

'Well, let's start with ten thousand. That should be enough for me to find a nice little place, not worry too much if I get this job or not, maybe hire a private detective to track down Micky.'

'Start with?' Mik queries, as he collects all the mugs and places them back on the tray. He picks up the plate and offers Jez the last biscuit. Of course Jez cannot refuse.

'Yeah, well, we'll have to see how it goes. I don't know how much a private dick will cost and I don't know if I can hold down a job now I'm sober.'

'Why do you think we'll give you any money at all?'

'Because you're dodgy. Both of you. Always thought Cal was anyway. Dead dodgy with all her extra shifts. Probably meeting her fancy man. Least that's what Micky thought.' He turns to Mik. 'Was it you?'

Now I do laugh, just the once. 'You really don't know Micky as well as you think you do.'

'I think I do, darling.' He sneers at me.

I shake my head slowly. Mik stands up and takes the tray away to the kitchen, he leaves the doors open and I hear him stacking the dishwasher, then switching it on. What the hell is he doing?

I'm beginning to get a headache and it's because I'm so tired. All this stress isn't good for me. I'm heavily pregnant, I could go into labour at any moment because of him. Although the baby would probably be fine I don't want him coming early; I want him to have the best chance possible. I couldn't bear to go through *that* again.

I pull my feet up under me, no mean feat considering how rotund I now am, and lean my head back against the sofa. I close my eyes as I begin to speak. 'We're not giving you anything, Jez. If you think we're dodgy, ring the police. Get them round here.' I open my eyes just as Mik enters the room; his eyes widen in alarm.

'Come on, Cal. Let's not be hasty. Don't make this difficult for us.' Jez really thinks he has the upper hand. Or is he bluffing? Just like me. 'I want cash,' Jez says. 'Not traceable then.'

'And just where do you think we'll get ten thousand in cash from? All the banks in this town have shut down in case you weren't aware. It's bank transfer or cashpoint machines. And do you know how many visits that would mean? And how many days?' I shake my head again. He's insane.

Jez smiles. He thinks he has me. Thinks that I'm giving it serious consideration.

Perhaps I am.

'Push off, Jez. I'm tired. Just leave. Go back to your own town. Are you still living in that bedsit above the offy?'

'Yeah. Used to be convenient but now I'm dry it's a temptation too far. So I have to move. Which brings us back to how much you're going to give me.'

'Nothing. Now leave.' I start to get up, which is quite an effort. Mik holds out a hand to help me but after the biscuit comment I bat his hand away and struggle up by myself. 'Come on, up you get, Jez. You're leaving.'

Jez cackles and rubs his eyes. 'Okay, Cal, have it your own way. But I'll be back tomorrow morning, so you can sleep on it.'

'We're not giving you anything, I've told you. Just go to the police.' I catch Mik wince as I say the words. I'm calling Jez's bluff. I just know that if we give him so much as a penny he'll be back time and time again and we'll never get rid of him.

'You're leaving, and don't come back. Not tomorrow or any other time.' I stand in front of him now, legs akimbo, hands on my hips.

'Don't suppose you could lend me a bit on account so I can get a nice hotel room.' He grins.

'Unless you could put me up? Nice big house this.'

I'm losing my patience now. 'Fuck off, Jez.'

'Very ladylike. Micky was right about you. Hard as nails.'

'Shut up and fuck off,' I say again, glancing behind me to see that Mik has sat back down and is trying hard to suppress a smile. What the hell is he playing at? He should be backing me up. He should be picking this snivelling little weasel up and flinging him into the street. Jez is no match for Mik physically.

'Let him sleep there,' Callie,' Mik says. 'It's getting late, dark outside.'

'What? No.'

Mik gets up now. 'Seriously, I'll deal with him. You go on up and get ready for bed. I'll soon have him sorted.'

I ignore Mik but speak to Jez again. 'Get up and get out,' I say between gritted teeth.

Jez shuffles his feet around a little, makes a feeble effort to get up then slumps back down. 'Been on my feet all day,' he says, his voice now pathetic. 'Early start too. Bus took forever. I won't be any trouble. We can carry on chatting tomorrow morning.'

Mik leans into me and snuzzles the back of my neck. 'Trust me,' he whispers. His action sends little tingles down my spine.

'Fine, whatever. Don't leave him on his own.'

Mik nods his agreement and smiles.

As I leave the room I hear Jez say to Mik, 'That's what she was like with Micky. Drove him bloody mad, she did.'

Upstairs I check on Jasmine, now soundly asleep. Her sweet little face, her chubby little hands, her soft breathing, all this comforts me a little. But I know I won't sleep so I run a deep bath and climb in. The bathroom is at the back of the house so I can't hear Mik and Jez. When I'm done I get ready for bed in the bathroom, then stand at the top of the landing listening for voices, but it's silent. Jez must have fallen asleep.

I climb into bed convinced I won't sleep but am just dozing off when Mik comes up. I leap up to a sitting position.

'What are you doing up here? I told you not to leave him.'

'Don't worry, he's not down there anymore. He won't be troubling us again. Trust me.'

'He's gone then?' I lean back into my pillows. 'Thank you. Thank you so much for dealing with him.'

Mik smiles, then sits down on the bed next to me and hugs me. 'Don't worry, I was not going to let him ruin our lives.'

'You didn't give him any money, did you? Even a fiver will bring him back for more. He'll know he's onto something then.'

'I didn't give him a penny.' He disappears to the bathroom and when he comes back he climbs in and cuddles into me. 'Sweet dreams,' he says, a smile on his face clearly visible before I turn off the light.

I shrug him off. 'I haven't forgiven you for the nasty comment about my size,' I tell him.

'You know I didn't mean it,' he says.

'Then why say it, especially in front of *him*?'

'It was for his benefit. And yours. I love you no matter what shape you are, you know that. I love that you're growing my son in there.' He wraps his arms around me again and I let him.

Rather surprisingly I go straight to sleep.

Twenty-one

Neither of us has mentioned Jez this morning. I'm pretending he never came here yesterday. Maybe Mik is too. I was up early and I've shampooed the chair he was sitting in, and cleaned the toilet he used. Now we're all sitting at the table eating breakfast with Jasmine when there's a loud knock at the door. It'll be Jez. Why won't he just give up?

I jump, but it's Mik who goes to answer. I close the dining room door behind him; I do not want Jasmine breathing the same air as Jez. Mik had better not allow him in here.

The door opens. Mik wanders in smiling.

'What have you done with him? I told you not to leave him alone.'

Mik frowns, then grins. 'It was the post,' he says. 'There's a little parcel for you.' He hands it over.

I'm suspicious. I'm not expecting anything. There really isn't anyone to send me anything. 'What is it? Who's it from?'

Mik laughs. 'I don't know. You need to open it.' He hands it over and sits down next to Jasmine, encouraging her to finish her toast.

I handle the parcel, more a fat letter really, with caution. I feel relieved when I see it's franked and not stamped, because Jez couldn't do that, could he? Actually, I'm being silly, Jez couldn't have sent a letter to me to arrive today, could he? I breathe out slowly as I fumble to open the package.

'What is it?' Mik asks casually. Has he bought me something lovely, a little piece of jewellery? After Jasmine was born he presented with a brand new wedding ring to replace the one Micky bought me. I wear it all the time obviously, and have now sold Micky's.

'Urgh,' I say, finally getting the contents out. 'It's a sample bottle.' I read the enclosed letter, a note from the surgery midwife to say that I forgot to bring a sample last week and they need one now. I'm to drop it in as soon as possible.

'I could do that for you,' Mik says, leaning over and reading the letter. 'Drop it in, I mean. I have to go out anyway.'

'Where are you working today?' I ask him, after we've cleared up breakfast. It's a weekday and he doesn't seem in any hurry to rush off.

'I'm not. I'm officially between jobs. I have a whole three days free.'

'Oh, yes, I'd forgotten what with all the Jez stuff.'

'So I've plenty of time to drop your sample off whenever you like.' He grins.

I've just put Jasmine down for her afternoon nap and I find myself staring out of my bedroom window looking up the street. I'm half expecting to see Jez come loping towards us, cocksure and full of himself. I have to remind myself that he doesn't know what we've done. He has no idea where Micky is and hopefully he'll never know.

I drag myself away from the window; I must not will Jez to appear, it's the last thing I want.

Downstairs Mik is finally back from delivering my sample and now has the house extension plans laid out on the dining table.

'Oh?'

'Thought I might make a start on the footings, since I've got the time off,' he says.

'Really? I thought we weren't going to bother.'

'No time like the present. I can start and take my time. Do it between paying jobs. But I could get all the footings dug then email the council to come and inspect them.'

I shudder. It brings back that stark memory on that dark, rainy night when Micky did what he did to me and we did what we did to him.

'You don't need to. We're not in any hurry, are we? Wait until after the baby's born.'

He doesn't reply. I glance over at him and he's just looking at me, his face pale, his eyes wide.

'What's wrong?'

'I think I need to start on the footings now.'

I feel my heart start to beat faster. That's not good when you're as pregnant as I am.

'W..w..why?' I stutter.

'You know why.'

I slide down onto a dining chair and gasp. Mik

runs off and fetches me a glass of water. He watches me take several gulps when he returns.

'Where is he?'

Mik is silent for too long.

'You don't want…'

'I do,' I cut in. 'Now just tell me.'

'In that old freezer in the garage.'

'Oh shit.'

'Don't worry, I've turned it on. He won't be, well you know, rotting.'

'Decomposing,' I correct.

'Yes, that.'

'What did you do to him?' I don't want to know but I *have* to know.

Mik does the silent thing again.

'Mik?' I urge.

'When he was asleep I just carried him into the garage and popped him in the freezer.'

'Didn't he wake up? How could he not have woken up? He's more alert than ever now he's not drinking and he was always a beady-eyed watcher.' I remember him propping up the bar alone in the pub before Micky came back from his holiday, his gimlet eyes were always darting everywhere, watching people, watching me.

'No, he didn't stir. He was out cold.'

'You didn't do something, like wring his neck?' I find myself imagining Jez's scrawny little neck inside Mik's strong hands. I'm ashamed to say I find the thought satisfying.

'No, no. I didn't touch him, well except for moving him.'

'I can't believe he didn't wake up. That's bizarre.'

'Not really.' There's a little grin on Mik's face. I can't quite believe what I'm seeing.

'What did you do?'

'I might have drugged him.'

'How, when?'

'In the tea.'

'But we drank the tea, it came from the same pot.'

'Not the same mug though.'

'No. What was it?'

'A bit of everything. The aim wasn't to kill him, just to render him unconscious. I emptied quite a few of those cold remedy capsules into his mug. He takes so much sugar that he never tasted it. I might have inadvertently dusted the biscuits with it too, that's why you couldn't have one. And he kept coming back for more tea so that made sure he finished off any dregs.'

'That's why he could hardly get off the chair. Was it enough to kill him?'

Mik shrugs.

'This is awful.' I start to cry; I think it's the pregnancy hormones because now I think about it, I really couldn't care less about Jez.

'I'm sorry. But I couldn't see any other way. You said yourself he would keep coming back. Callie, I'll do anything for you, for us, for our family, to keep us safe.'

'I know.' And I do know, and I would too.

'Do you think he froze to death?'

Mik shrugs.

'Hypothermia,' I say, scanning the room for my

phone. I grab it from the sideboard. 'I'll Google it.'

Mik waits with his usual patience. How I love this man.

'Yeah, he froze to death,' I say, after scanning pages of information which is more concerned with warming someone up.

'Of lack of air.'

'Suffocated. I didn't think of that. Is he still in there? Have you checked. Knowing him he woke up and got out.' I imagine him climbing out, ringing the police, waiting for them as we sit here discussing him. 'What about his phone? Is it in there with him? Will it still work? He wouldn't even need to climb out, just ring from inside the freezer.'

Mik shakes his head. 'No phone, no keys.'

'Where are they? His phone could be traced to here. When they start looking for him they'll come straight here.'

'I took it from his pocket last night. I turned it off. After I'd dropped your sample off at the doctors' I turned it back on.' He grins now. 'Then I drove out of town and hurled it in the lake.'

'Which lake?'

'Does it matter? I don't know. The one many miles away and on his way home.'

'Was it still on when you threw it in?'

He laughs. 'It was still on, but the battery was at five percent, so it probably isn't now. If it survived the water. I threw the keys in too.'

'Okay.' We should be fine, I think it unlikely anyone will even look for him, but Mik did the right thing, he always does the right thing. 'You're sure he hasn't escaped?'

'He's still in there. Frozen solid. Anyway, I locked it. The key's on a hook in the garage. He couldn't have got out even if he woke up.'

'No. Good. You know what this makes us?'

Mik shakes his head slowly.

'Serial killers.'

'Not you. Just me,' he says, looking into my eyes.

'Yeah.' I can't look at him, so I get up and leave the room.

I don't know what to think, not consciously anyway, but deep down inside I'm pleased. Isn't that awful? I'm pleased that Jez won't be turning up and making demands and implied threats. I'm pleased that he won't be instigating a search for Micky. I'm pleased my man has looked after me, us.

Twenty-two

He's finally here, our little boy. Two weeks late and weighing almost two pounds more than little Jasmine did. Ironic really that after all that stress with Jez and me worrying I might go into early labour, he was late.

'He's amazing,' Mik says, hugging his little bundle wrapped in blue.

'No more after him.' I mean it too. Absolutely no more. He is such a bruiser that he tore me far more than Jasmine did. I can't chance another.

Mik looks at me and smiles. 'Absolutely,' he agrees. 'I'll get the chop asap.' He makes a scissor gesture with his fingers.

I laugh. He says asap because I told him Micky always said that. It used to annoy me when Micky said it, but I love it when Mik does. Weird, eh?

We've only been home a couple of hours and I'm exhausted. We're lying on our bed and Jasmine is lying between us. She's not asleep but is happy and content, she's cuddled her little brother and now she's a little bored by him.

'Do you want to call him after your uncle?' We've discussed this a few times and not come to any decision. I have no male relatives to name him after but I know Mik was close to his uncle.

'Second name,' he says. 'You choose first.'

I narrow my eyes at him, he knows why.

'Sorry. You choose *the* first.'

'Never slip,' I say, smiling and yawning at the same time.

'So many things to never let slip,' he echoes.

Later, when we're downstairs, Jasmine is asleep in her bedroom and our new baby, now named Oscar Joseph, is full of milk and sleeping in his crib next to the sofa. Mik's uncle was Yusuf but we've Anglicised it. Not that it would matter much now with Jez no longer being a problem. But we don't want any hints, anything that might put a question in someone's mind.

The new extension, the one we were in no hurry to build, is coming on a treat. The walls are already waist high. Mik no longer digs everything himself, he uses machines now, because he can, so everything is quicker. And he gets help when he needs it. His business is very different now to how it was when we first met. That's what being legitimate and legal does, gives you credibility, lets people trust you.

I have no idea where Jez is under those walls. And that's the way I like it. See no evil and all that.

However, I feel in fairness to Mik, who I know is carrying the burden of Jez's demise on his own, I am going to own up to something. I've decided tonight is the night. Maybe it's the baby hormones, maybe it's guilt, or maybe it's to even up the score, to make Mik feel better.

He brings me a cup of tea as well as one for himself and sits down next to me. He gazes over at a sleeping Oscar.

I take a breath.

'I have a confession to make.'

He turns and looks at me with alarm. Then waits, because that's who he is, a patient man.

'Well, we did what we did with Micky together. We really don't know exactly who… you know… finished him. It was a joint action. But Jez wasn't.'

Mik looks at me, sadness in his eyes. He shakes his head slowly. 'I felt I had no choice.'

I reach over and put my finger to his lips. The last thing I want is for him to feel worse than he does or feel he has to justify what he did. I know why he did it and I fully support him. It was Jez's own fault; he just wouldn't leave us alone. And he would never have left us alone no matter how much money we gave him.

'I know.' I grip his hand. 'I know you did the best for us, all of us.'

He nods his head slowly, but doesn't say anything.

'I killed my mum,' I blurt out.

He looks at me, alarm showing on his face.

'I put her out of her misery.'

'Oh Callie,' he says, gripping *my* hand now.

'Don't say anything, just listen. I have to say it then never mention it again. She was ill, as I've told you. A series of strokes had left her so ill, she couldn't move her left side at all and she couldn't speak. She could scribble a few words on a notebook I'd got her but the effort exhausted her. I asked her if she was in pain and she wrote YES YES YES. The effort of that made her close her eyes. She was still at home then; I was looking after her but I was struggling. The nurse from the surgery came out and that last time she called the doctor who arrived within half an hour. He didn't stay long though and didn't say much either other than that Mum had to go to hospital right away so they could *make her comfortable*. Mum gurgled something that sounded like no, not that anyone took any notice. He got on the phone then, started making arrangements. An ambulance would come sometime, he said. Then he left. And the nurse stayed and looked at us both with pitying eyes. It was horrible.'

'You don't have to say any more,' Mik says.

'I do. Mum started making the gurgling noise again and looked over at the notebook which had been moved away from her by the doctor. I grabbed it and gave it to her but she didn't write anything. Instead she looked at the nurse and widened her eyes. Anyway, the nurse got the message and made an excuse about going to the toilet and suggested a nice cup of tea. I said I'd love one and suggested she make it. When she'd gone out of the room Mum wrote in the book.' I take a deep breath now because what she wrote is still hard for me to think about.

Mik shakes his head but he doesn't speak.

'She wrote KILL ME. And I knew I would have

to. I waited until the nurse came back from the toilet and ushered her into the kitchen and pointed at the kettle and showed her where everything was, including the biscuits and told her to help herself. Then I went back in to Mum who looked at me and pleaded with her eyes. I took a cushion and held it over Mum's face. Obviously I didn't want the nurse to know but I also didn't care if I got caught because this was about Mum and it was what she wanted.' There are tears running down my face now. But I'm determined to carry on. 'It took a long time, despite her being so ill and not able to move much, it must have been five minutes but it felt like an eternity. It's not like it is on TV where people kick their feet twice then they're gone. Mum made a horrible noise and I wondered if I should stop but then I remembered that look in her eyes, so I didn't.'

Mik grabs me and hugs me to him. I continue talking into his chest.

'Then the nurse came in with the teas on a tray, she'd made one for Mum too, in a beaker with a spout, like a baby cup. But none of us drank that tea. I don't know if she knew what I'd done but she was very nice and closed Mum's eyes and gave me a hug and then she cancelled the ambulance. And later the doctor came back and wrote the death certificate and eventually Mum was taken away. I never saw her again.' I'm properly crying now; remembering is very upsetting but it had to be done. Mik has to know that he's not alone. 'I had no choice, you see, just like you didn't. Now we're even. So you're no more guilty than I am.'

He folds me further into his hug.

'I am,' he says so quietly that I almost don't hear him.

'No, you're not,' I say into his chest, my voice muffled by his jumper.

He lets me go and moves slightly away before glancing over at Oscar again.

'There was a man,' he starts, his voice quiet, his eyes staring into the middle distance. 'We were hidden in the back of a lorry on our way here, boxes built around us like a wall. It was good but it wasn't perfect; we had to be careful. The driver had told us if he banged on the partition then we had to be silent. He banged. But there was a man. He'd fallen out of the truck when we'd climbed in. Hurt himself badly. A big cut on his leg, a broken arm I think and he'd banged his head, it was bleeding from the back. He was bad. We were desperate to get him to a hospital but we had to wait until we got here, the UK. I was sitting next to him; he was leaning against the boxes. I kept feeding him little sips of water throughout the journey which must have been eighteen hours or more. But we were near the checkpoint before the ferry. He was groaning. I whispered to him to stop. It was dark but one of the others shone a mobile phone light on him. He looked bad. His eyes were wide and staring. And he was groaning and groaning. The driver banged again and one of the others hissed, 'Shut him up.' Then because I was nearest to him I got a sharp dig in the ribs and a thick scarf was thrust into my hands. I used it to muffle the sounds he was making but he wouldn't stop. The driver banged again and I pressed the scarf over the man's mouth. Still he groaned. I pressed harder. Then he stopped.' Mik stops and looks at me.

'You had no choice,' I say.

'Probably not.' He looks away again. 'I was seventeen. I'd seen so much misery and death by then. Seen my family killed. Now I was a killer. I never even knew that's man's name.'

'What happened to him? When you got here, I mean.'

'No idea. We got out of the lorry and never looked back. I was taken to a place agreed with my uncle. I told him about it and he said it wasn't my fault and I liked to believe that.'

'He probably wouldn't have survived anyway. It was probably already too late by then, even if you'd got him to a hospital.'

'My uncle said that.'

'My turn to hug you now,' I tell him.

'I haven't finished.'

I can't imagine there's any more to say about this poor man but I wait in silence because that's what Mik does.

Eventually he takes a deep breath and lets it out in a long sigh. 'I killed my uncle.'

'But you weren't even there when he died.'

'I was. I did it the night before they called. They obviously didn't check him until long after I'd left. He was so pathetic lying there, thin and coughing and not knowing who he was or where he was. He looked so miserable, so sad. He was crying all the time on my last visit. Just crying and repeating over and over, help me, help me. So I stroked him, calmed him, hugged and rocked him, then I laid him down. He actually smiled up at me. First time I'd seen a smile from him in a long time. Then I put my hand over his mouth and nose and I kept it there. It didn't take long. I sat with him for a long time after, held his hand. Then I tucked him up in bed, turned the light off and left him. On the way out I told the staff that he was asleep.'

I'm stunned. Then I say, 'You had no choice. You did the right thing.'

'I had a choice. I could have let him go on crying and begging for help. But no one came, no one helped him. He just lay there repeating it over and over.'

'You had no choice.'

'No.'

'But *we* have a choice,' I say, trying to sound jolly. 'We have to live for him. And for my mum.' I don't add not for Jez or Micky, but Mik understands it. Because he understands me just as I understand him.

We're very alike, Mik and me.

Psychopaths, maybe.

'You do know how much I love you,' I say, wrapping my arms around his neck and kissing him on the cheek over and over, giggling.

'Me too,' he says, sounding shy. 'Fell in love with you the first time I saw you watching me from the window. Knew we'd be together, whatever it took.'

I stop kissing him and pull back, scrutinise his face. That was long before Micky did what he did to me and we did what we did to him.

'Me too,' I say, resuming my kissing.

Like I said, we're very alike, Mik and me. Very.

THE END

Someone's lying. Is it her husband or her best friend?

Recurring dreams of a car crash make sleep a nightmare for Juliette but the real nightmare begins when she wakes up. Her devoted husband Robin stays by her side, determined to help her remember how her whole world was turned upside down.

He's the love of her life and he's vowed he will never leave her and he's true to his word. But there are things that Robin doesn't know so she turns to her best friend Stephen to find out the truth. He's the brother she never had and they've been best friends since childhood. He knows her like no one else, not even Robin.

As Juliette's memory begins to return she starts to doubt her own sanity and is forced to ask herself – do we ever really know the people we love?

As children they were inseparable...

Born less than a year apart, siblings Adam and Angie are twins in all but name. Inseparable as children, as adults they still spend every weekend together and it seems that nothing can come between them. Adam, a world-famous artist with a lifestyle to match, is happy to share his success with Angie and they live as they've always done; Adam and Angie against the world.

Until the day that Adam meets the love of his life.

Enigmatic and charming, Perry walks into Adam's life and Angie watches helplessly from the side lines as her brother is taken away from her. Adam and Perry whirl around Europe without a care in the world and now Adam is too busy for Angie, too busy for his friends, too busy for anyone or anything but Perry.

Adam has a new life now. With Perry.

Printed in Great Britain
by Amazon

26229497R00118